She had a mons
and her ears we
the explosion.

Lindsey sat on the examining table, her bare legs dangling beneath the short hem of the hospital gown. Dan stood beside her, where he'd been almost the entire time since she'd arrived. It had been a near miracle that neither she nor anyone else was seriously injured.

Finally the doctors allowed Dan to drive her home. Reluctantly listening to his orders and taking her medicine, she said, 'There. Are you happy?'

He gently lifted a hand to the bandage on her forehead. 'How can you even ask me that when you look like this?'

A wave of warmth flooded through her, making her knees weak. It was hard to be sensible and levelheaded when he said things like that. When he looked at her that way.

Then he abruptly stepped back. 'Now, get into bed. You need to rest.'

'Fine.' She surrendered with a yawn. Lindsey just wished she knew exactly what lay behind Dan's tender solicitations. Friendship—or more?

Dear Reader,

A warm welcome to Special Edition!

We kick-off with *The Not-So-Secret Baby,* a wonderful THAT'S MY BABY! story from Diana Whitney. And look out for more baby fun next month with *That's* Our *Baby!* Talking of babies, Muriel Jensen is back by popular demand with another WHO'S THE DADDY? story, *Daddy To Be Determined*.

Gina Wilkins continues her HOT OFF THE PRESS trilogy where three small-town reporters are suddenly tangling with love. *Bachelor Cop Finally Caught?* will be followed by the final instalment, *Dateline Matrimony*, in September.

The fascinating conclusion to Laurie Paige's THE WINDRAVEN LEGACY is *When I Dream of You*. While Christie Ridgway brings us the Prince Charming of every woman's dreams in *From This Day Forward*, and Laurie Campbell raises some interesting paternity questions for her rugged hero in *Home at Last*.

We hope these Silhouette Special Editons make *your* summer even more special.

The Editors

Bachelor Cop Finally Caught

GINA WILKINS

For Sally, still crazy after all these years.

First published in Great Britain 2002
Silhouette Books, Eton House, 18-24 Paradise Road,
Richmond, Surrey TW9 1SR

ISBN 0 373 24413 4

23-0802

Printed and bound in Spain
by Litografia Rosés S.A., Barcelona

GINA WILKINS

is a bestselling and award-winning author who has written more than fifty books for Silhouette. She credits her successful career in romance to her long, happy marriage and her three 'extraordinary' children.

A lifelong resident of central Arkansas, Gina sold her first book to Silhouette in 1987 and has been writing full-time since. She has appeared on several bestseller lists. She is a three-time recipient of the Maggie Award for Excellence, sponsored by Georgia Romance Writers, and has won several awards from the reviewers of *Romantic Times Magazine.*

Chapter One

Twenty-six candles blazed on the birthday cake in front of Lindsey. A roomful of people crowded around the table at her friend Serena's to watch her blow them out. All too aware of the one person who wasn't there—Dan Meadows—she drew in a deep breath and efficiently extinguished all the tiny flames. Her audience applauded enthusiastically.

"Happy birthday, Lindsey." Serena Schaffer North, the party's hostess, gave her friend a quick hug as she spoke.

Lindsey responded warmly. "Thank you. It's a great party, Serena."

"It is, isn't it?" Visibly satisfied, Serena cast a quick glance around the roomful of chattering, laughing guests. "I'm so glad everyone could make it."

Not everyone, Lindsey couldn't help thinking.

As if she'd developed a sudden, disconcerting talent for mind reading, Serena said, ''I wish Dan was here. He said he would try.''

''He's probably out beating the bushes for clues about the firebug.''

''Probably.'' With a frown, Serena shook her head. ''I hope he catches the guy soon. Dan's starting to look so stressed lately. Frankly, I think he needs a vacation.''

''So do I.'' Lindsey remembered the lines that were slowly carving themselves around Dan's eyes and mouth. Dan needed more in his life than his work. He needed a reason to go home at night.

So did she.

Serena's husband of almost three months, Cameron North—Lindsey's boss and editor at the newspaper—joined them just then, sliding his arm around his wife's waist. ''Aren't you going to have any of your own birthday cake, Lindsey? You'd better hurry or those vultures will eat it all up before you get any.''

''Someone will save me a slice.'' Not particularly concerned about the cake, Lindsey studied the quiet contentment on the faces of the couple in front of her.

Serena and Cameron had met under extraordinary circumstances—she'd found him lying on the side of a road, beaten half to death, with no memory of who he was or how he'd gotten there. Just about five months later they were married. Cameron had recovered most of his memories of his past, but he had told Lindsey without embarrassment that, as far as he was concerned, his life hadn't really begun until he'd awoken in a hospital room to find Serena leaning over him.

Though she'd teased him about being a sentimental softie, Lindsey had actually been touched by Cameron's confession. She'd also been aware of a ripple of envy. Serena and Cam had known so quickly that they were right for each other. How could it have been that easy?

Okay, so she knew it hadn't been *that* easy. She had seen the way Serena suffered during the weeks that Cameron had gone back to Texas to rediscover his past, before he'd come to the realization that this was where he wanted to spend his future. But it certainly hadn't taken him twenty years to learn to appreciate what had been right in front of him.

Determined not to waste any more of her birthday moping over Dan, she pasted on a bright smile and playfully demanded that someone bring her a slice of her birthday cake. She laughed when at least six people immediately thrust plates of cake in front of her. She had lots of friends, she reminded herself. A job she enjoyed. The freedom to pursue her dreams wherever they led her. And if the romantic dream that had led her back here wasn't meant to be—well, she'd find a new dream somewhere else.

Twenty years was long enough to invest in a fantasy that she was beginning to believe was never meant to come true.

The following morning, as she did on the rare Saturday mornings when she wasn't working, Lindsey made a haphazard attempt at housework, zipping through the house in which she'd grown up, a dust cloth in one hand and a broom in the other. She'd inherited the three-bedroom house three months ago, when her father had passed away after a lengthy illness. He'd died on the Monday after New Year's Day, a sad holiday this year—just as Christmas had been, since he'd been becoming weaker and weaker. Lindsey's many friends in Edstown had made sure she'd spent little time alone during the holidays.

Her older brother, B.J., a career military man, had insisted that the house should be Lindsey's as she'd spent the past two years living there and taking care of their father. Even though she'd argued that she'd done so only because she wanted to, B.J. had refused to accept part ownership of the house, settling, instead, for a portion of the modest insurance settlement.

During the past couple of weeks, Lindsey had been thinking about putting the house on the market. When it sold, she would insist that B.J. accept part of the proceeds. She could take a job in a bigger market—Little Rock, Atlanta, maybe Dallas—where she could start a new life. She had the credentials, the ambition, a few connections. There was nothing holding her here now.

Nothing at all, she thought with a wistful little sigh.

Her doorbell rang just as she finished running the vacuum cleaner in the living room. Glancing down, she wrinkled her nose at her appearance. Oversize green T-shirt, baggy denim shorts, fuzzy purple house shoes. Her hair stood in messy red spikes around her smudged face. She looked like an orphan from the cast of *Annie,* she thought with a shake of her head. Hoping her caller was a salesperson or a close pal rather than her minister or the mayor's wife—neither of whom she was expecting—she opened the door.

As it had for the better part of twenty years, her heart tripped when she saw Dan Meadows on her doorstep. As she had since she'd gotten old enough to understand the meaning of the word "pride," she hid her reaction behind an impudent grin. "Well, hey, Chief. Whazzup?"

Dressed in an oatmeal-colored cotton sweater and a pair of faded jeans, he eyed her skimpy attire. "Lose your calendar? It's the first week of March, not the middle of summer."

"I've been cleaning," she said with a shrug.

"Ah. That explains your new perfume. I thought you'd switched to Eau d'Pine."

Wrinkling her nose in response to the bad joke, she opened the door wider and motioned for him to enter. "Since the place is clean, you might as well come in."

"How could I resist that gracious invitation?" Pulling his right hand from behind his back, he handed her a wrapped package as he passed her. "Happy birthday, Lindsey. Sorry it's a day late."

Kicking the door closed behind him, she studied the pretty paper and the jaunty bow. "No way you wrapped that. It's too pretty."

"You're right. I had it wrapped at the store."

"It's almost too fancy to open."

He grinned. "What makes you think there's anything inside? Maybe the pretty package is all I got you."

"And maybe you're full of hot air."

Laughing, he ruffled her hair—exactly the way he had when she was a kid tagging at his and her brother's heels. His nine-inch advantage over her five-foot-three height made it even easier for him to treat her like a kid. ''Just open the present, princess.''

His use of the childhood nickname made it difficult for her to keep her smile in place. ''Yeah. Sure.''

With the ease of someone who'd spent a lot of time in this house during the past twenty years, Dan settled on the couch, an arm draped across the back, his legs stretched in front of him. His chestnut hair tumbled over his forehead, ending in a fringe just over his dark brown eyes. He looked tired, and there was a slight touch of gray at his temples now, but Lindsey could still see traces of the handsome teenager he'd been in the roughly good-looking man he had become.

She sat in a nearby chair, the gift in her lap. Though she usually ripped into her presents at light speed, she opened this one with excruciating slowness—just because she knew it would drive Dan crazy.

''You're going to have another birthday before you get into that,'' he complained, as she'd known he would.

''I want to savor the moment. You're usually giving me grief instead of presents.''

''I give *you* grief? You're the gung-ho reporter who stays on my heels all the time looking for a hot lead—as if there's all that much to report in Edstown.''

''Just doing my job, Chief.''

''Yeah, well, you sure as hell make it tough for me to do mine sometimes.''

Because this was an old and generally unproductive argument, Lindsey let the comment pass as she peeled the last bit of paper away from the box. A moment later she swallowed a lump in her throat so she could say, ''Dan, it's beautiful. Thank you.''

His smile was just a bit smug. ''Do I know what you like or what?''

Yes, he knew what she liked—when she was twelve. She had collected unicorn figurines from the time she was a little girl until she'd gone off to college. Her room had been filled with them, the walls covered with unicorn posters. Now Dan had bought her a blown-glass unicorn for her twenty-sixth birthday. Somehow he'd completely missed the fact that she was no longer the little girl he'd known so long ago.

Her heart aching, she set the unicorn—a perfect symbol for hopeless fantasies, she reflected glumly—on the coffee table. ''Have you had lunch? I was just about to eat.''

''As a matter of fact, I'm starved. What've you got?''

''Sandwiches.''

''Just what I had a craving for,'' he drawled.

With a weak laugh, Lindsey led the way into the kitchen. They spent the next half hour munching ham-and-Swiss-on-rye sandwiches, pickle spears, and raw vegetables with ranch dip. During the casual meal, they talked about her brother—Dan's best friend since adolescence—and their mutual friends in Edstown. She asked about his parents, who were, as usual, spending the winter at an RV park in southern Texas; he assured her they were fine, that he'd spoken to them only the day before.

There were a couple of subjects they carefully avoided, such as the arsonist who'd been eluding the local authorities. And then there was the one topic neither of them *ever* mentioned—Dan's bitterly unpleasant divorce two and a half years ago, barely six months before Lindsey had moved back to take care of her father. Even if Lindsey had wanted to bring up his marriage debacle—which she didn't—Dan would not have cooperated. He'd forbidden everyone to even mention his ex-wife's name in his presence.

"So, anyway, the noise Mrs. Treadway reported hearing outside her window was nothing more than a broken tree branch tapping against the glass. Unfortunately, by the time we managed to find that out, Jack and I were wet to the bone, covered in mud, half-frozen, and we'd narrowly escaped being midnight snacks for Mrs. Treadway's rottweiler."

Lindsey winced even as she laughed at Dan's wryly told anecdote. "So you had a close encounter with Baby, did you?"

He all but shuddered. "Baby missed biting me in a very sensitive area by an extremely narrow margin. I swear I felt his hot breath right on my—"

"I get the picture," Lindsey said quickly. There were some mental images she wasn't prepared to deal with right now—Dan's "sensitive areas" among them. "Baby's not as bad as he pretends to be. Around Mrs. Treadway, he's just a big, dopey puppy."

"Yeah, well, thanks to Baby I almost had to switch from the bass section of the church choir to the soprano section."

She smiled and nodded toward his empty plate. "Would you like anything else to eat? I have some leftover birthday cake that Serena insisted I bring home.''

''Cake sounds good, if you have an extra slice.''

''I have plenty,'' she assured him and rose to cut him a piece.

''I'm sorry I had to miss your party. I got tied up at the station and didn't get away until after eleven.''

''Which explains the dark circles under your eyes.'' She studied his face as she set the dessert plate in front of him. ''You aren't getting enough rest lately, Dan. Serena thinks you need a vacation.''

''She does, does she?''

''When's the last time you took more than twenty-four hours off?''

He shrugged. ''It's been a while,'' he admitted. ''But I won't be taking a vacation anytime soon—not with some crackpot trying to burn down every building in the damned town.''

''He usually waits a few weeks between hits. You should have time to take a break while the other investigators pursue leads.''

''That's the thing—we *have* no leads,'' Dan growled. ''The guy's slick, I'll give him that. He's not leaving clues.''

''He'll screw up—and when he does, you'll catch him.''

''Yeah, but that means he'll have to strike again first. We've had one death because of this guy so far. I don't want anyone else endangered, including our firefighters.''

''You'll catch him,'' Lindsey predicted again.

''Damn straight. But not if I'm off on a vacation. Besides, who takes vacations this time of year?''

"People who are tired and need a rest?"

Dan only shrugged and filled his mouth with another forkful of cake.

"This has been nice," he said a few minutes later, when his plate had been cleaned and the last sip of iced tea drained. "You and I haven't had a chance to sit down and talk much lately—not without you holding a notebook in your hand, anyway."

"No. You've been so busy we've hardly seen each other since B.J. was home for Dad's funeral."

The mention of her late father made Dan's smile dim a little. "So, you've been doing okay? Living here by yourself, I mean."

"I'm fine," she answered gently. "I miss my dad, of course, but he was so ill and so debilitated that I knew he was ready to go. And I've been on my own before, you know. I lived alone for three years before I moved back two years ago to take care of Dad."

"You let me know if you need anything, you hear? I promised B.J. I'd keep an eye on you."

Her teeth gritted. "Thanks, but I'm quite capable of taking care of myself."

"Of course you are." He glanced at his watch, which kept him from seeing the way her brows dipped in response to his slightly patronizing tone. "As much as I've enjoyed this, I've got to go. I have things to do at the station."

She walked with him to the door. "Try to go home at a reasonable hour tonight," she advised him. "You won't be doing anyone any good if you collapse from exhaustion."

He chuckled and reached out to ruffle her hair again. "You sound just like my sister."

''Well, I'm *not* your sister, and if you do that to my hair one more time, I'm going to sink my teeth into your hand.''

The snarled threat only made him laugh. ''Now you *really* sound like my sister.''

Clenching her teeth tightly together, she opened the door, then forced herself to say pleasantly, ''Bye, Dan. Thank you again for the birthday present.''

''You're welcome.''

Some impulse made her speak, just as Dan started down the front steps. ''I'm thinking about selling the house.''

He stopped and turned to look at her in obvious surprise. ''No kidding? Why? Is it too much for you to keep up?''

''No. I can handle the maintenance. I'm considering looking for a job in a bigger city. Dallas or Atlanta, maybe.''

''Oh.'' He shoved his hands in his pockets, looking as though he didn't quite know how to respond. ''Well...I can see where you'd have better career prospects in a bigger market, but...you'd be missed here.''

She noted that he didn't say who would be missing her if she left. ''I haven't really made a final decision yet. I'm just mulling it over.''

''I see. Well, you do what you think is best for your future. I've gotta go, okay? See you around.''

''Yeah.'' Lindsey leaned against the doorjamb and watched him climb into his car. ''See you around, Dan.''

Sometime later she carried the unicorn into her bedroom and set it on the dresser. Her childhood collection had been packed away since she'd left home for college—not that Dan would know that. It had been years since he'd seen the inside of her bedroom.

He probably still pictured ruffles and teddy bears, she thought glumly.

Stupid man.

She caught a glimpse of herself in the full-length mirror attached to one of her closet doors. A low groan escaped her as she studied the grubby clothes that dwarfed her petite figure, and the fuzzy house shoes that would have looked more at home at a teen slumber party. She ran a hand over her spiky hair and glared at the smudge of dust on her unpainted cheek.

''No wonder he still thinks I'm twelve,'' she muttered. She winced when she remembered his ex-wife, with her perfect hair, perfect face, perfect teeth, perfect breasts. Lindsey turned sideways and poked out her chest, eyeing the results in the mirror. ''Pitiful,'' she grumbled. ''Just pitiful.''

She mentally replayed the way she'd bantered with Dan, swapping put-downs and bad jokes, pretty much the way she and her brother carried on when he was home. When they met on a professional basis, she and Dan usually ended up yelling at each other—and she'd admit that she usually started it. Maybe it was just a teensy bit her fault that he hadn't seen her as a sexy, desirable woman.

If she gave up now and moved away, putting her dreams behind her, would she always regret not giving it one more try? She'd never been a quitter, and had never been hesitant to go after something she wanted—except for Dan. What did she have to lose—except her dignity, her pride and her ego?

The grubby woman in the mirror suddenly looked a little pale, but there was a new look of determination in her green eyes.

Dan Meadows was about to find himself with a brand-new problem on his hands.

Chapter Two

"What are you doing here already?" Dan's secretary said, glaring at him from his office doorway.

He looked up from the paperwork littering his desk and said, "Excuse me?"

"I heard you didn't leave here until after ten last night. Now here it is not even eight in the morning and you're already at it again." Hazel Sumners shook her head in exasperation. "You are not Superman, Dan Meadows. You need rest."

He heaved a gusty sigh. "I'll have you know I got nearly eight hours' sleep last night. That's plenty of rest for a grown man."

"Rest involves more than a few hours of sleep," she scolded. "How about leisure time? You know—fun? You didn't even take time off for Lindsey's birthday party Friday night."

"I saw Lindsey on Saturday," he retorted. "I didn't totally ignore her birthday."

"That isn't the point. You should have been at that party having a good time with your friends. You should have taken off Saturday afternoon to go fishing with Cameron, and a few hours yesterday for church and a nice Sunday dinner somewhere. But what did you do? You worked, except for having a quick sandwich with Lindsey."

"How did you—"

"I saw Lindsey at church yesterday morning, and I asked her if she'd seen you during the weekend. She told me you popped in to tell her happy birthday and then came right back to the office."

"Do you ask everyone about my business, or just a select few?" He kept his tone mild, but he couldn't help being a bit annoyed that Hazel had been monitoring his actions so closely. Her job was to keep up with his work schedule, not his personal life.

"Your friends are worried about you, Dan—and so are your co-workers. You're working too long and too hard, and if you don't slow down you're going to crash just as hard."

It was with some effort that he held on to his patience. "I'll take some time off as soon as we catch whoever has been setting fires around here."

Still scowling, she shook her spray-stiffened, salt-and-pepper head. "This is just like those break-ins that took all your time last summer. You said that as soon as you solved those, you'd take a vacation. But Delbert Farley's been in jail for weeks now and you're still working just as hard as ever. Catch this firebug and something else will come up. And before you know it, your whole life will have passed you by.''

''Thank you so much for that cheery prediction. Now perhaps you could go answer the phone before it rings right off your desk?''

She turned and stalked away, mumbling something about foolish, stubborn men.

Unable to resist the cliché, Dan shook his head and muttered, ''Women.''

What was going on with them these days, anyway? Lately it was either his secretary ragging him about his working hours, or his women friends nagging him to take a vacation. Concerned grandmas complaining about the blessedly few serious crimes that took place in Edstown, or his sister calling him to fuss about not making enough time for his family. Not to mention Lindsey—nipping around his heels one minute for every detail about his ongoing investigations…and then announcing out of the blue that she was considering moving away.

What was she thinking? Sure, she'd managed well enough in Little Rock for a couple of years before she'd moved back here. But she was a small-town girl at heart, not one of those tough, big-city reporters. And frankly he wouldn't want to see her turn into one.

Not that she cared about that, of course. She hadn't asked for his opinion. She'd simply stated that she was thinking about putting her house up for sale. It was actually none of his business—even if he *had* promised her brother that he would keep an eye on her now that their father had passed away.

He'd known even as he'd made the promise that it

was only a formality. Though ten years younger than Dan and B.J., Lindsey was still a grown woman, fully capable of making her own decisions. If she chose to move to Dallas or Atlanta—or Antarctica, for that matter—there was little anyone could do to stop her. Certainly not someone who was nothing more to her than a long-time friend of her older brother.

Oddly enough, considering how often Dan complained about her hanging around so much in her professional capacity, he would miss her if she moved away.

Forcing his concentration back to his work, he glanced at the files littering his desk. They contained summaries of the fires that had been set around town—starting with the old dairy barn last summer. A few weeks after that, a recently vacated rent house had burned, under strikingly similar conditions. An old garage a few weeks after that. And then the tragic cabin fire—the one in which Truman Kellogg had died.

Kellogg had been asleep when the fire started and he'd died in his bed—probably never woke up, mercifully. None of the other suspicious fires had involved buildings that were occupied. Of course, there was the possibility that the arsonist hadn't known anyone was there: Truman had rarely visited his vacation cabin and then usually only during summer months.

There had been other details about that fire that differed from the others, but it was hard not to be suspicious about it, considering everything that had been going on in the past few months. Neither Dan nor the fire chief had ruled out arson in Kellogg's death, though they had no proof that the fire had been deliberately set—not like the others, in which there were obvious signs of arson yet no clue about the arsonist.

There'd been a long gap between that fire and the next one—the abandoned warehouse last week. Long enough that people had begun to hope the fires had ended. At least no one had died in the latest fire. Dan was determined to catch the guy before anyone else died.

"Chief?" Hazel's voice came through the desk intercom, her clipped tone letting him know she was still annoyed with him. "The mayor's on line one."

Dan reached for the phone, knowing that *this* caller wouldn't be nagging him about taking a vacation. The mayor would be quite content for Dan to work twenty-four hours a day if it meant putting a quick and quiet end to this increasingly troublesome arson problem.

"Do something with it."

In response to the reckless order, Paula Campbell put her hands on her ample hips and studied Lindsey curiously. "And just what would you have me do with it?"

Eyeing her reflection in the beauty-shop mirror, Lindsey shrugged. "I don't know. Cut it. Curl it. Fluff it. Just do something so I don't look like a twelve-year-old boy."

Paula chuckled and reached for a towel and a cape. "No one would mistake you for a boy. Not with those pretty, big green eyes of yours—or that perfect skin. But if you want a softer look than that shaggy style you've worn for so long, we can certainly take care of that. You want to flip through some style books?''

''No. I trust you to know what looks good. Just make it a style I can maintain without a lot of fussing, okay?''

''You got it.'' Intrigued by the challenge Lindsey had just presented, Paula set to work with enthusiasm. ''What's inspired this makeover, anyway? Someone you're trying to impress? Some *male?*''

Painfully aware of the women listening openly from the three other stations in the four-operator salon, Lindsey responded with a laugh that she hoped was credibly casual and derisive. ''Yeah, sure, I'm hoping Brad Pitt will leave his wife and find me on the streets of Edstown. Can't a woman change her hairstyle without being accused of trying to catch a man? I've just had a birthday—isn't that reason enough to want to make a change?''

''Well, sure—especially a momentous birthday like thirty or forty or fifty. But you just turned twenty-six, not exactly one of those numbers that usually send women running for a makeover or a facelift. So I figured it must be a guy.''

''Too bad your new boss is already taken, heh, Lindsey? That Cameron North is one fine-looking man,'' the woman being tinted and permed in the next chair murmured.

Lindsey smiled. ''He's definitely good-looking—and definitely taken. He and Serena are the most blissful newlyweds I've ever been around.''

Lila Forsythe sighed wistfully from beneath her helmet of hair rollers. ''Their story is so romantic. The way she saved his life—the way he fell in love with her before he even recovered his memories. Serena's mother thinks it was love at first sight, you know. That's why she wasn't worried that they got married so quickly."

"Love at first sight." Paula snorted as she spun Lindsey's chair around so she could lower her to the sink for a hair washing. "I've hardly ever seen it work out. Maybe Serena and Cameron will be the exception."

Lindsey kept her mouth shut. She had no intention of confessing that her own experience with love at first sight had lasted twenty years and counting. She could just imagine Paula's response to *that* scenario.

She only half believed it, herself. Maybe she was just in the *habit* of being in love with Dan Meadows, rather than actually *in* love with him. But if she left town without at least trying to find out for sure, she suspected that the question would haunt the back of her mind for the rest of her life.

Dan thought of Lindsey again during lunch, which consisted of a deli sandwich at his desk. Hazel had brought him the sandwich when she returned from her own lunch break, and had then spent five minutes lecturing him about his work habits before he'd sent her away so he could eat in peace.

He'd spent the past two hours in an intensive meeting with the fire chief and two arson investigators from Little Rock. A pile of new notes littered his desk now, but the meeting had actually accomplished very little. The consultants had looked over every scrap of evidence on the Edstown fires, including a long visit to the most recent crime scene, but the conclusions they'd drawn hadn't been much different from what Dan and Fire Chief John Ford had already figured out. Someone around here was deliberately setting fires and covering his tracks so well there was no way to tell who he was. Yet.

Pushing a hand through his brown hair—which felt shaggy to him, reminding him he needed to make time for a cut—he wondered how long it would take Lindsey to come snooping around in an attempt to find out everything that had been said in the meeting. He'd have to be suitably vague—resulting, he hoped, in an article that the locals would find reassuring. He was sure they'd be glad to know that arson experts had been consulted—he just wouldn't tell them the experts hadn't provided much assistance so far.

Sure enough, it was less than an hour later when Hazel buzzed him. "Got a reporter here from the *Evening Star,* Chief. Are you in?"

Hearing the dry humor in her voice, he knew the reporter was aware that Dan was in. He could still say no, of course. But he might as well get this over with. "Yeah, Hazel, send her in."

He pushed his hand through his hair again and made a halfhearted effort to straighten his desk, making sure no confidential paperwork was visible. He wouldn't put it past Lindsey to snoop through them when he wasn't paying close attention.

But it wasn't Lindsey who ambled into his office a couple of minutes later. This was a man—young, tall, lanky-limbed, a lazy smile gracing his squarish face and reflecting in his cool-gray eyes.

"Well, hey, Riley," Dan drawled, telling himself he wasn't really disappointed that it wasn't Lindsey.

One reporter was just like another one, he assured himself. ''Is Lindsey busy bugging the fire chief? The mayor, maybe?''

''Lindsey took the day off.'' Riley O'Neal arranged himself loosely in one of the chairs on the other side of Dan's desk. ''Cam sent me to find out if there are any leads on the arson story.''

''Lindsey took the day off?'' Dan repeated, surprised. ''Is she sick?''

''Not as far as I know. Some people have lives outside their jobs, you know.''

The barb was delivered with a grin. Like everyone else in Edstown, Riley was well aware of the police chief's workaholic tendencies—although it was hardly a trait Riley shared. Riley's philosophy was to do exactly as much work as necessary to survive, and to spend the rest of his time taking it easy.

Thirty years old, Riley had been working on a novel—or claimed to have been—since he'd graduated from college. He hadn't grown up in Edstown, but his maternal grandparents had lived here, as did a favorite uncle who still maintained a home here. Riley had visited often enough as a boy that nearly everyone knew him even before he took the job with the local newspaper. He asserted that he liked the slower pace of small town life. Made it easier for him to find time to write, he'd explained.

Dan had always considered Riley a bit of an eccentric, a borderline loner, and a wiseass to boot—but for all of that, he rather liked him. Besides, Riley wasn't nearly as pushy a reporter as Lindsey was, which made it easier to deal with him when Dan wasn't in the mood to cooperate with the press.

So there was no reason at all to be disappointed that Riley had shown up when Dan had been expecting Lindsey. After all, if Lindsey moved away, Dan would have to get used to working with other reporters from the local paper.

He would miss her, he realized again, even as he answered Riley's questions about the arson investigation. Lindsey was practically family to him. So it made perfect sense that the thought of no longer having her in his life left a rather hollow feeling inside him.

"So you're no closer now to solving these arsons than you were a month ago?" Riley asked, his pen poised over the battered, reporter's notebook he'd pulled from his jacket pocket. "And have the charges officially been upgraded to murder since Truman Kellogg died in that fire two months ago?"

Deciding he'd better concentrate on his answers before he slipped up and said something stupid, Dan pushed thoughts of Lindsey to the back of his mind and gave his full attention to Riley, reminding him that there was no proof yet that the Kellogg fire was linked to the others. Riley would let him get away with that—Lindsey would have kept pushing. Dan couldn't help smiling wryly at the thought...and realizing again that he would miss her when—if—she left.

Holding the tip of her tongue between her teeth, Lindsey leaned close to the lit makeup mirror, an eyeliner gripped in her right hand. She swore when her hand twitched, smearing liner across her right cheek. "I can't do this."

Connie Peterson laughed and handed Lindsey a moistened makeup-remover pad. "Of course you can do it. It just takes a little practice—something most women do before they reach your age, by the way."

Lindsey scowled, making it more difficult to remove the smudge. "I haven't had time to mess with makeup. I've just slapped on mascara and blusher and lip gloss, and that always seemed like enough."

"So why have you decided to change that now?" the makeup consultant, whom Lindsey had known since high school, asked curiously.

"Oh, you know…getting older. Trying not to show it." Lindsey hoped her answer was suitably vague and believable.

Connie's laugh came perilously close to a snort. "Yeah, right. You hardly look old enough to drive legally. I bet you still get carded every time you order a drink."

Keeping her eyes fixed on the mirror, Lindsey painstakingly followed the directions Connie had given her for applying the eyeliner. The effort was a bit more successful this time. "So maybe I'd like to look my age."

"It's a guy, isn't it?"

Lindsey's hand jerked again, resulting in a matching liner smudge on her other cheek. She reached for the remover again. "Why does everyone assume I'm changing my appearance for a guy?"

"Because we've all done it," Connie replied with a smirk. "You've got a great new hairstyle, and now you're investing in war paint. Definitely a guy."

"*You've* changed your appearance to try to attract a guy?" Lindsey eyed the brown-haired, brown-eyed woman curiously. Attractive and extroverted, Connie had always seemed so comfortable around men, always having a date for local events, and rumored to have bruised a few hearts during the years. Lately she'd been deeply involved with a man from a neighboring town, and there was broad speculation that this time it was starting to look permanent.

"Oh, sure. Remember when I tried bleaching my hair my senior year in high school? *Major* mistake—but I did it because Curtis Hooper said he liked blondes."

Lindsey couldn't help laughing. "Curtis Hooper? No kidding? I didn't know you ever had a thing for Curtis."

"Yeah, well, how was I to know he meant he liked blond *men?*" Connie shook her head in self-derision. "He really was cute. But maybe I should have gotten a clue, when the only thing he and I really had in common was that we both enjoyed putting on makeup?"

"You think?" The shared humor relaxing her, Lindsey decided Connie's feminine insight might come in handy, as long as Lindsey was careful about how she worded her questions. "So, have you ever seen it work? A woman changing her appearance to get a man's attention, I mean."

"Oh, sure. Lots of times. A guy gets used to seeing someone a certain way, you know? Then when she makes a change, he starts looking at her in a different way—sometimes as if for the first time."

Which, of course, was exactly what Lindsey was hoping for, though she had no intention of admitting that at the moment. "It doesn't seem...well, a little desperate to you?"

Connie laughed. "Heck, no. Sometimes you just gotta hit 'em over the head, girl. Men just don't get subtlety."

"I heard that," Lindsey muttered with a sigh, remembering all the subtle messages she'd sent Dan in past months. Messages that had apparently gone right past his thick male head.

"I don't suppose you want to tell me who it is you're trying to catch?"

Lindsey shook her head and answered gruffly. "Never mind about my reasons. Just teach me how to use this war paint, will you?"

"That's my job." Connie reached cheerfully for a mascara wand. "By the time I get through with you, you're going to knock that guy—whoever he is—right off his feet."

Lindsey was beginning to believe this entire day had been an exercise in humiliation. But she wasn't a quitter. She'd started this, she might as well finish it. "What color lip liner should I use? And why the heck do my lips need lining, anyway?"

At six o'clock Friday evening Dan was helping two of his officers subdue a couple of angry and belligerent drunks in the parking lot at Gaylord's, a bar-and-Cajun-food establishment on the seamier side of town. It was earlier than usual for this type of altercation. He'd gotten in on it only because he often dined at Gaylord's on Fridays, and he had arrived just in time to see a drunk take a swing at one of his officers. His presence signaled a quick end to the commotion, and he watched in satisfaction as the two brawlers were subdued and hauled away.

He was greeted the moment he walked into Gaylord's by the burly owner who worked behind the bar. "Hey, Chief, how you doing?" Chuck shouted over the manic zydeco music blaring from numerous speakers.

"Fine, thanks, Chuck. How's the gumbo tonight?"

"Same's always. Best you ever put in yo' mouth. Find yourself a chair and I'll send Gary over with a bowl. You want a beer with that?"

"Better make it water. I'm still on duty."

"You always on duty, eh, Chief? I'll send some corn fritters with your gumbo. Save room for dessert now, you hear? Mama's been baking all afternoon, and I'll make you a pot of fresh chicory coffee."

"You don't have to twist my arm." Looking forward to the first hot meal he'd taken time for in several days, Dan crossed the scarred hardwood floor to his favorite booth, a small one in the back just big enough for two. He intended to dine there alone, as he usually did.

He certainly didn't expect to be joined almost immediately by Lindsey Gray.

It took him a moment to realize it *was* Lindsey. She looked different somehow...and it had little to do with the red glow from the strings of chili-pepper-shaped plastic lights hanging over their heads. She'd changed her hair—it looked softer, a bit curlier. And she was wearing more makeup than usual. She didn't need it, of course—but he had to admit she looked great.

Only then did he notice what she was wearing. It

was a long-sleeved knit dress—unusual in itself for Lindsey—and it was cut up to here and down to there. Not a lot up top to flaunt, but what was showing looked good. And her legs—well, who'd have thought a woman so short could have legs that long?

"Hi, Dan. Fancy meeting you here." The voice was definitely Lindsey's—unexpectedly husky for such a little bit of a thing.

"Lindsey. What are you doing here? Do you, uh, have a date or something?"

"No," she answered, and he wondered why he was glad to hear it. "I'm just in the mood for company and Cajun food tonight."

"Will my company do?" He motioned toward the other side of the booth, managing at the same time to glare at a greasy-looking guy who was checking out Lindsey's legs from a table nearby.

Lindsey hesitated just long enough to make his scowl deepen. So how come she was taking such a long time to answer? Had she been hoping to hook up with someone else tonight? Was that the reason she'd dressed to thrill? Did she *like* being ogled by greasy goofballs on the make? "Sit down."

Lifting a freshly plucked eyebrow in response to his growled command, she slid onto the other bench. "I don't want to intrude if you want a quiet dinner alone."

Though he wasn't entirely sure he bought the excuse, he answered, "I always enjoy visiting with you. You know that."

Her dimples flashed in a smile that made her look more like B.J.'s gamine little sister than the sexy redhead who'd greeted him a moment earlier. ''Very nice. What did you order?''

''Gumbo. Want the same?''

''Sure. Why not?''

Catching Chuck's eye, Dan held up two fingers. Chuck responded by making a circle with his thumb and forefinger.

Knowing the food would arrive eventually—service here being dependable if not overly speedy—Dan tried to think of a conversation opener. ''So...how's your week been? I haven't seen you around much.''

''I've been busy. And so have you, I hear. Riley said he's had to practically chase you down whenever he had a question for you.''

''Yeah, what's with that, anyway? How come Riley's suddenly covering my office?''

Lindsey shrugged, one shoulder almost emerging from the deep neckline of the black dress. ''I've been working on a series of features we're going to run next week. They're about the town's oldest five citizens. It's been fascinating.''

''Did you talk to Marshall Collier?''

''Of course. He's 102—and still sharp as a tack. He tells great anecdotes.''

''And Nellie Pollard? You couldn't interview her.''

''That was a bit more challenging,'' she admitted. ''Poor thing just sits in a chair and rocks and hums all day, when she's not sleeping.''

''So what did you do?''

''I interviewed her one surviving son. And her grandsons. Then some of the people she gave piano lessons to during her years as a music teacher—her life reflected through the lives she touched.''

''Did you feel you got to know her that way?''

''I sat with her for a while yesterday,'' she said. ''The song she hums all the time? It was her favorite—one she taught all her students. Her husband sang it to her the night he proposed to her. She hasn't played piano since I was in diapers, but she still hears that song in her head.''

''That's pretty sad.''

''I know. She's been in a steady decline for the past ten years. But for the almost sixty years prior to that, she brought music into the lives of several generations of young people. Now a lot of them are old, too—but they remember her music.''

Dan studied Lindsey's face in the glow of the chili-pepper lights. She looked…dreamy, he thought. As if she could hear the music playing even now.

He had no doubt that the articles would be good. Better than should be expected from the average small-town newspaper. But then, the *Evening Star* was better than the average small-town paper, he conceded—especially now that Cameron had become managing editor, and as long as Lindsey and Riley wrote most of the articles. Cameron would stay—after all, he'd married the paper's owner. But Riley would be leaving eventually, once he decided to get serious about that book he'd been writing for so long.

As for Lindsey—well, she probably *should* be utilizing her talents in a bigger market—as much as Dan hated to admit it.

Chuck's son, Gary, appeared then, bearing a heavily loaded tray. Two big bowls of rice, two of spicy seafood-and-vegetable gumbo. A platter of warm corn fritters. Two mason jars filled with ice water.

"You guys don't want beer with this?" Gary asked, setting the food in front of them.

"No."

"Yes."

They'd spoken simultaneously. Dan glared at Lindsey. "No," he repeated.

She frowned, but shrugged. "No," she said to Gary.

"Whatever. Give me a sign if you need anything." Gary shuffled off at his usual speed—a mosey.

"I'm on duty," Dan said in response to Lindsey's questioning look.

"I'm not."

He spooned gumbo over his rice, then added a liberal dash of hot sauce. "Since when do you drink beer?"

"I don't very often. But sometimes it's good with Chuck's gumbo. I *am* of age, Dan—want to see my ID?" she asked a bit too sweetly.

He knew very well that she was old enough to drink legally—which didn't mean he had to like it. How often did she show up here like this, anyway—dressed this way and drinking beer?

He was seeing an all new side to B.J.'s little sister—one he wasn't sure he liked. But then, Dan had never liked change.

They ate in silence for a few minutes—until their meal was interrupted by a big-shouldered young man with a shock of brown hair, his blue eyes focused squarely on Lindsey's petite, but prime, cleavage.

"Hey, Chief," the intruder said without looking at Dan.

"Hey, Jimmy. What's up?"

"Not much. How you doing, Lindsey? Haven't seen you around in a while."

She responded with her usual friendliness. "Hi, Jimmy. How are things at the muffler shop?"

"Lot better now that Delbert Farley's behind bars. I always hated working with that as—that jerk."

Dan found it extremely irritating that Jimmy's gaze had hardly wavered from Lindsey's neckline. "It was good to see you, Jimmy," he said abruptly, not caring if he sounded rude. "Enjoy your dinner."

"Oh, uh...yeah. See ya, Chief. You, too, Lindsey."

"See you, Jimmy." Lindsey waited until Jimmy was out of hearing distance before commenting to Dan, "You're in a mood tonight."

"What do you mean?" he asked a bit too sharply.

"See? You're snappy. And I'm not even hassling you for a story."

He shrugged. "Sorry. Guess I'm just hungry."

She smiled a little and nudged the platter of corn fritters toward him. "So eat."

Their hands brushed when he reached for one. Even as he reacted to the contact—not quite a static shock, but a similar feeling—he noticed that she'd had a manicure, her usually unvarnished nails now sporting a dark polish.

For some reason the observation made him frown again.

Chapter Three

Her makeover had been a massive waste of time, Lindsey decided glumly. The primping, the fussing, the shopping—all for nothing. Dan hadn't even noticed.

Trying to feign enthusiasm for the food, she finished her meal.

"Do you want anything else?" Dan asked.

She shook her head. "Thanks, but I couldn't eat another bite."

"I'll see if I can get the check, then." Dan lifted a hand, trying to catch the young man's attention. "Seems like Gary's moving slower than usual tonight."

"I've noticed that, myself. I wonder if he needs vitamins."

Chuckling, Dan shook his head. "I think he's just slow."

"I'll pay for my own meal, of course."

Shooting her a glance over his coffee cup, Dan replied flatly, "You will not."

"Look, I didn't join you so you could buy my food."

"Lindsey—I'm buying. Now drop it."

She hated it when Dan used the same voice her brother used when he was annoyed with her. Dan wasn't her brother, damn it. But it seemed as though there was nothing she could do to change his perception of her—which meant she'd blown a few hundred dollars worth of hairstyling aids, cosmetics and a great new dress.

"Hi, Lindsey. Looking good tonight." A lean cowboy in a flashy red shirt and sprayed-on jeans strolled past the booth, tipping the Western hat he hadn't bothered to remove as he sent Lindsey a slow smile.

Her feminine ego had needed that boost. She smiled back at him. "Thanks, Bo. How's it going?"

"Can't complain. Save me a dance later?"

"Maybe."

The vague response seemed to satisfy him. He touched his hat again, nodded a greeting to Dan, then sauntered on.

Dan was wearing another frown. "Someone you know?"

She was tempted to point out how silly the question was, since she'd spoken to Bo by name, but considering that Dan wasn't in the best mood, she merely replied, "We went to school together."

"Were you expecting to see him here tonight?"

Lifting her eyebrows in response to the inquisition, she answered a bit coolly, "No."

"This isn't really a great place for a single young woman to hang out on a Friday night. Especially later in the evening when the booze has been flowing for a few hours. We get a lot of calls out here on weekends."

Drumming her painted nails on the scarred tabletop, she replied, "Perhaps I should remind you again that I am an adult? And this is one of the few places around here for single young adults to hang out."

He held up a hand, a peacekeeping gesture that did little to appease her. "Just making a comment."

Nothing about this evening had gone the way Lindsey would have liked. She might as well have stayed home in her T-shirt, shorts and fuzzy slippers. She could have crashed in front of the TV and dined on chips and dip. That would have spared her the humiliation of having Dan sitting right across the table, totally oblivious to the changes she'd made during the past week, lecturing her as if she were a naive high school student.

Sure, Jimmy and Bo seemed to find her attractive—but face it, those two were attracted to anything with breasts. It was Dan's interest she'd hoped to catch tonight—but not like this.

Throwing some money on the table, Dan glanced at his watch. "I need to run by the station for a few minutes. I'll walk you to your car."

"Who said I was ready to leave?"

Dan went still for a moment. "You're through eating, aren't you?"

She glanced toward the dance floor, which was just starting to come to life. "Yes, but I'm not necessarily in a hurry to get home. There's nothing waiting for me there."

"So you're going to do what? Hang out here drinking beer and dancing with cowboy Bob? Is that why you got all gussied up tonight with the hair and makeup and the low-cut dress?"

So he *had* noticed the changes. And this was his way of acknowledging it—not as a compliment but a criticism. She slammed both hands on the table. "His name is Bo. And, yes, maybe I'll dance with him. Maybe I'll even sleep with him. Heck, I could have a quickie with him out in the parking lot and then come back for a tumble with Jimmy."

Her quietly furious outburst made Dan's jaw clench, his eyes going hard and narrow. "Just what the hell is your problem tonight?"

She stood and leaned over the table, making sure he had a good view of what Jimmy and Bo had seemed to find intriguing despite her small size. "My problem is that I've grown up, Dan Meadows. And it seems like just about every guy in this town has finally figured that out—except for you."

Before he could come up with an answer, she straightened and smoothed her dress, trying to get a grip on her temper. "Thanks for dinner. Now I'll let you get back to work—I'm sure that's where you'd rather be, anyway."

She turned on one heel and walked away without looking back. A group of singles was beginning to gather in the far corner of the big room, laughing, flirting, drinking and dancing. It wasn't Lindsey's usual type of entertainment, but maybe it was time for her to make some changes. She'd spent the past two years taking care of her father and fantasizing about Dan. But her father was gone, and now she was tired of sitting in her house alone, waiting for something that was obviously never going to happen.

Bo saw Lindsey approaching, grinned and pulled out a chair. The music was louder in this corner, as were the patrons, so he practically had to yell for her to hear him. "Have you ditched the chaperon?"

Chaperon. That was exactly the way Dan had been acting, Lindsey mused angrily. Or like an older brother. "Yeah, he's gone," she agreed without looking around to make sure that was true. "You said something about a dance?"

Bo promptly stood, dropped his hat on his chair and ran a hand through his dark hair. "Yes, *ma'am.*"

She wasn't really planning to sleep with Bo—or anyone else—tonight. But there was no need for Dan to know that. It was none of his business how she chose to spend her Friday evening. And that was his choice, she reminded herself.

Damn the man.

Dan was still seething late the next afternoon. Every time he thought about Lindsey—too many times in the past few hours for his peace of mind—he got mad all over again.

What had gotten into her last night? In all the years he'd known her, he'd never seen her act that way. Never heard her talk that way.

He could still see her leaning over the table, green fire in her eyes, a flush of temper on her face, the gaping neckline of her sexy black dress revealing slender, creamy curves that he was male enough to appreciate. He felt vaguely guilty about the number of times he'd mentally replayed that picture…not to mention the unwanted stirrings of response he felt every time he did so.

Hell, he was no better than Jimmy or cowboy Bo, practically drooling over her—even worse, because he was old enough to know better. He'd known Lindsey Gray since she was in pigtails, damn it.

She wasn't a little girl now.

He might have followed that line of thought a bit further, but he was distracted just then by his work.

Someone had called in another fire.

Lindsey showed up at the scene, of course, a camera around her neck and a notebook in her hand. It annoyed Dan greatly that for the first time her presence distracted him from his work. He had never allowed that to happen before—and he was impatient with himself for doing so now. It had to be because he was still perturbed with her behavior last night, wondering what she'd been trying to prove.

She still looked different, he noted as she marched toward him, her reporter's look of determination on her face. Her new haircut made her coppery hair lie more softly around her face than the choppy style she'd worn before. Her green eyes were highlighted again by judicious use of cosmetics, and her stubbornly set mouth glistened with a light coat of shiny gloss. Instead of her usual jeans and sweatshirt, she wore a soft-looking, heather-colored mock turtleneck and close-fitting black slacks with black boots.

She looked like a classy, competent, professional woman, he realized abruptly. A far cry from the grubby urchin he'd once known so well. Even as he reluctantly admired the woman, he found himself missing the urchin.

Sidestepping a water hose, Lindsey stopped in front of Dan. "Looks like they wrapped it up quickly."

He nodded. "We were fortunate this time. A delivery driver saw the smoke from his van and called it in. The fire trucks arrived before the fire had spread from the kitchen to the rest of the house."

Lindsey turned to survey the smoke-darkened back of the frame bungalow. "You're certain this fire has nothing to do with the arsonist you're looking for?"

"Yeah. Mrs. O'Malley went next door to visit her neighbor, got distracted by a television program over there and forgot she'd left something cooking on the stove. I came by to make sure, of course, as soon as I heard there was a fire run in this neighborhood, because it's in the same general area as the arson fires, but I'm convinced this was totally unrelated."

She nodded and made a note in her pad.

As the firefighters gathered their equipment in preparation to leave, Dan let his thoughts wander away from work again. "You look...well rested," he said to Lindsey.

"I was home before ten last night," she said a bit curtly. "Alone. Are you happy?"

He didn't understand the distance that seemed to be developing between them—and he didn't like it. Maybe it was his fault. He cleared his throat. "Listen, you were right about last night. It was none of my business if you wanted to stay and have fun with your friends."

She didn't seem at all mollified by his concession. In fact, it only seemed to annoy her more. "Well, gee, thanks. I'm so glad I have your approval. Now I can just go party my toes off without a second thought.''

With that she turned and stormed away, apparently intent on interviewing the resident of the damaged house.

Dan stared after her, utterly bewildered. ''What the...?''

''Are you and Lindsey at it again?'' a woman's asked in wry amusement from behind him.

He turned to find Serena North, her hands on her hips, her head tilted to one side as she studied him. ''Serena,'' he greeted her. ''What are you doing here?''

''I heard about the fire, so I came by to check it out. Mrs. O'Malley is a good friend of my mother's.''

''She's fine. Upset and embarrassed, of course, but it could have been much worse. As it is, she only gutted her kitchen. She could have lost the house had the fire not been called in so quickly.''

''Poor dear. I'm sure Mother will be here soon to help out.''

Dan found himself watching Lindsey again, noting how sympathetically she seemed to be dealing with the distraught older woman. ''What's with her, anyway?''

Serena frowned in confusion. ''Mrs. O'Malley?''

''No, Lindsey,'' he answered impatiently. ''Has she been acting strangely around you recently?''

''Not that I've noticed. She's made a few changes in her appearance, of course, but every woman does that periodically.''

''It's more than her appearance. It's her attitude.

Seems like she's had a real chip on her shoulder for the past week or so. Maybe it's just around me.''

Serena smiled. ''I don't see anything new about that. You and Lindsey are always squabbling. You telling her she's getting in your way, her insisting that as a reporter she has a right to be in the middle of everything.''

Dan should have found that admittedly accurate description reassuring, but somehow he didn't. ''I think it's more than that. She just doesn't seem like herself.''

Turning to study Lindsey, who was now talking to the fire chief as he prepared to depart, Serena looked momentarily concerned. ''I'm sure she's still adjusting to the loss of her father, even though it had been expected for a long time. It couldn't have been easy for her, losing both parents within five years, and Lindsey still so young. Maybe it would be easier for her if B.J. was around more, so she wouldn't feel so alone.''

''She's hardly alone. She has more friends than anyone in town.''

''That isn't the same as family. You know that.''

Was that Lindsey's problem? Was she missing her parents, her brother? ''Maybe that's it. I'll try to take it easier on her.''

Serena laughed and patted his arm. ''Start treating Lindsey like a poor orphan and she's liable to tear off a layer of your skin. She'll work this out in her own way, Dan.''

''And if that means moving away? She's talking about selling her house, you know. Moving to a bigger news market, like Dallas or Atlanta.''

Serena frowned for a moment, then smoothed her expression with a little shrug. ''I hadn't heard that, but I guess it doesn't really surprise me. There isn't anything to hold her here now that her father's gone. There are definitely more prospects for her—career-wise and socially—in a bigger city.''

''Socially?''

''Well, of course. There aren't that many single men her age around here. I've heard her say she'd like to marry someday, start a family—she loves children, you know. Not every woman can be as lucky as I was and find the perfect guy literally lying in her own backyard,'' she added with a slight smile.

Dan was still struggling with the image of Lindsey married with children. His first instinct was that she was too young—but then he remembered that she'd just passed her twenty-sixth birthday. Where had the time gone?

He tried to picture her with some of the single men in town—specifically, the two who'd seemed so interested in her at Gaylord's last night. Jimmy and Bo. Neither of whom were even remotely right for Lindsey. Nor was any other guy who sprang to his mind just then.

Her interview with the fire chief completed, Lindsey closed her notebook while Dan watched. With a little wave to Serena that might have been meant to include Dan, she walked to her car, which she'd parked in a line of others at the curb.

Was she walking differently? Adding a little sway to her hips that hadn't been there before? Or was he just noticing she walked that way? Maybe it was the boots. Or maybe he was spending too much time focusing on Lindsey when he should be concentrating on his own business, he thought irritably, deliberately turning away. He changed the subject abruptly, suggesting to Serena that they should go talk to Mrs. O'Malley.

Serena immediately agreed, and Dan went back to work—though he felt the questions about Lindsey hovering at the back of his mind, waiting to nag him when he was alone again.

Maybe he *did* need a vacation.

Edstown wasn't known for its social opportunities, but there were three events that locals turned out for faithfully—the Independence Day celebration in July, the Fall Festival at the beginning of October and the March Mixer. The origins of the latter had grown fuzzy with time, but the mixer had been held every year since the late 1940s. Now a fund-raiser for the Community League, the event generated revenue for a variety of local charities. Prominent citizens and city leaders—the chief of police among them—couldn't even consider missing the mixer, and of course Lindsey attended to cover the evening for the newspaper.

Usually she looked forward to the gathering. This year she was tempted to call in sick.

She didn't, of course. She dressed in one of her new outfits—a form-fitting emerald-green dress with spaghetti straps and a floating asymmetrical hemline. Paired with backless heels, the dress gave an illusion of height that she liked. She needed that little ego boost tonight.

Fluffing her coppery hair around her carefully made-up face, she decided she was as ready as she was going to be. Unfortunately, it was a cold, damp night, making a coat necessary. The closest thing she owned to a dress coat was a lined gray raincoat. Since her only other choices were the leather jacket she wore most days or a puffy parka reserved for really cold weather, she chose the raincoat. She would shed it quickly when she arrived, she decided. Maybe she would shop the after-season sales for a nice coat for next winter—wherever she happened to be by then, she thought with a sigh.

She was slipping out of the raincoat even as she stepped into the brightly lit and colorfully decorated community center. Rows of coat racks served as an informal cloak room. She hung her coat on an empty hook, leaving nothing of value in the pockets, since there would be no attendant. She smiled at the two women sitting at a table strategically placed across the hallway to block the entrance into the ballroom. "You two got ticket duty tonight, hmm?"

"Only for the first hour," Marjorie Schaffer replied with a smile for her friend Virginia Porter. "We're taking shifts."

"Good idea. I'm sure you have impatient dance partners waiting inside."

Both widowed and in their early sixties, the older women laughed, blushed a little, then took Lindsey's ticket and urged her to go on in.

Because Lindsey had stalled so long getting ready as she'd tried to work up enthusiasm for the evening, the ballroom was already crowded when she walked in. She estimated that she knew by name at least 75 percent of the people there, and it seemed as though they all tried to greet her at once.

Compliments flew, along with quick barely touching hugs and smacking-air kisses. ''You look fabulous!'' ''Love your hair, dress, earrings, shoes.'' ''Have you been working out?'' Though large, fancy parties weren't her first choice of entertainment options, Lindsey considered herself pretty good at dealing with them. She could schmooze and mingle like a skilled socialite when necessary.

The same couldn't be said for all her friends. Though Serena and Cameron looked perfectly at ease, Riley seemed to be in danger of falling asleep at any moment. And Dan, when she spotted him, might as well have been one of the security guards who'd been hired for the evening. His faintly vigilant posture, the politely professional expression on his face, his conservatively cut dark suit—all marked him as a man who was here as part of his job, not because he particularly enjoyed such gatherings.

When he saw her, Riley rather abruptly disengaged himself from the two giggly teenagers who'd been testing their flirting skills on the good-looking, unconventional reporter. With his characteristic rolling saunter, he made his way easily through the crowd, coming to a stop in front of Lindsey. Hands on his lean hips, he gave her a slow once-over. ''Damn,'' he drawled. ''You look *good.*''

She giggled like one of the teenagers. ''Thanks. Did someone forget to tell you this is a dressy occasion?''

Lifting an eyebrow, he looked down at his own outfit, which consisted of a blue-and-cream checked-cotton shirt, worn unbuttoned over a cream-colored T-shirt and khakis. ''What do you mean?'' Riley asked with feigned innocence. "I'm even wearing socks."

"Oh, so you are. For you, that counts as formal wear, doesn't it?"

He extended an arm to her. "Dance with me. It will keep me from falling into a coma."

"Not the most flattering offer I've had in a while," she chided, laying her fingers on his surprisingly muscular forearm. "Are you asking me to dance only because you're so bored?"

Fully aware that she wasn't really offended, he chuckled as he escorted her to the dance floor, where a good number of other couples swayed to recorded dance music. A new number was just beginning, and Riley turned Lindsey into his arms, comfortably taking the lead. Riley had always been a good dancer. She allowed herself to relax and enjoy.

"So what's with the new look you've been showing off the last couple of weeks?" Riley asked, proving once again that very little escaped him despite his carefully cultivated air of lazy unconcern.

She shrugged one almost-bare shoulder. "I just decided it was time to start looking like a grown-up."

He made a face. "Why would you want to do that? You're not even thirty yet."

Lindsey smiled up at him. "Who said you have to be thirty to be grown-up? You're thirty and I wouldn't exactly call you a model of maturity."

"Oh, gee, thanks. So why'd you suddenly decide it was time for your metamorphosis?"

"Just ready for a change, I guess. In a lot of ways."

"I've heard rumors that you're thinking about selling your house. Maybe moving away."

Even though she'd mentioned the possibility to only a few people, she wasn't surprised Riley had heard. Word traveled fast in Edstown, and Riley had a way of staying abreast of the latest gossip—though he would have heatedly denied being in the least interested, of course. "It's a possibility."

"Thinking about jumping back into the fast lane, hmm?"

"I just need changes," she repeated. "Don't you ever get…restless? Itchy?"

"Itchy?" His grin turned wicked. "Sounds to me like what you need is a sex life."

"I just need a *life*," she retorted flatly. "Of any kind."

"Well, as happy as I would be to offer my services in certain areas, I know you too well. You're the kind who gets involved with a guy and you start thinking permanence. Commitment." He gave a dramatic shudder before adding, "Kids."

He was right, of course. Lindsey was the traditional type at heart. Marriage and children had always been in her plans. Unfortunately, her long-time obsession with a man who gave little indication of returning her interest had kept her from looking seriously in other directions. It was probably time for that to change, too.

With a bittersweet smile, she replied, "No offense, but I can't see the two of us having babies and growing old together. So, as fond as I am of you, we'll stay just friends."

"I'll have to defer to your wisdom. Even if you do look incredibly hot in that dress."

Because he sounded sincere enough about the compliment to give her a completely feminine little thrill, she went up on tiptoes to kiss his cheek. "If a no-strings, ungrown-up affair was what I wanted, you would be at the very top of my list," she assured him.

"I'll take that as a compliment."

"It was intended as one."

The music came to an end. Riley released her, but laid a hand on her arm to keep her still for a moment. "Seriously, Lindsey, if you need to talk, you always know where to find me."

"Thanks, Riley." She smiled at him, then turned away—only to find herself face-to-face with Dan, who didn't look at all happy with her.

She and Dan hadn't exactly parted on the best of terms earlier, she remembered. And it had been her fault, she admitted now. She'd been prickly and defensive, and she couldn't expect him to understand why. She was the one who had suddenly changed. Dan hadn't been acting any differently than he ever had—which, of course, was exactly why she was upset with him. It was no wonder he was watching her now as if he wasn't sure what to expect from her.

She managed to smile at him. "Hi, Dan."

"Hi." Someone bumped him from behind as the dance floor began to fill again. Dan reached out to take Lindsey's arm and walk with her to the side of the room, out of the way. "Are you having a good time?"

"So far, but I haven't been here long. How about you?"

"Oh, you know. This isn't really my sort of thing. Mostly I'm here because I'm expected to be."

"You'd probably rather be at your desk."

He seemed about to agree, then he smiled a little and shook his head. "To be perfectly honest, I'd rather be fishing."

She placed a hand on her heart. "Why, Dan Meadows. You mean there's actually something you like as well as your job?"

"I'm not quite the hopeless workaholic everyone thinks I am."

The music started again—another slow song. Across the room, chattering townspeople gathered around the heavily laden refreshment tables. There would be live entertainment and drawings for door prizes later in the evening, but the first hour was set aside for visiting, dancing and munching. The event primarily provided an excuse for the locals to dress up and mingle, raising money for good causes in the process.

This crowd differed from the one she'd seen at Gaylord's last night, of course. This was a somewhat more sedate gathering, with no alcohol served, so she didn't expect to see Bo or Jimmy there. It wasn't at all their style.

"Do you want something to eat?" Dan motioned toward the tables.

"No, not yet. Dance with me."

He looked startled by her impulsive invitation. "Uh…dance?"

"Sure, why not? C'mon, the song's just starting."

"I'm not much of a dancer. Not like Riley."

She caught his hand and tugged. "Dance with me, Dan."

Though he still looked doubtful, he allowed her to lead him back on the floor.

Dan wasn't a bad dancer, she quickly discovered. Just a stiff one. Holding her several inches away from him, he rested his right hand sedately at her waist and held her right hand loosely in his left. He would have danced just this way with the minister's wife, Lindsey thought in exasperation, and deliberately moved a little closer to him.

After a few moments of silence, she tilted her head back to look up at him. ''Do you remember the last time we danced together?''

Dan seemed to be counting musical beats in his head. ''It's been a while.''

''It was five years ago—on my twenty-first birthday. My family threw a surprise birthday party for me at the country club. They hired a band.''

Dan had attended the party with a date. Melanie. She of the perfect hair, teeth and breasts. Melanie had made little secret of the fact that she would rather have been just about anywhere other than at a college girl's surprise party, and she hadn't liked it at all when Dan had given Lindsey a brotherly birthday kiss after their dance. At least, Lindsey supposed he'd intended it as a brotherly kiss. It was a lot more than that to her. She'd replayed that kiss during a hundred daydreams afterward.

Three days later Dan and Melanie had eloped. And Lindsey's young heart had been broken.

Was she really willing to go through that again?

Did she really have any other choice?

''I remember,'' Dan said.

She doubted his recollections very closely mirrored hers. She wondered if thoughts of that night brought back painful memories of Melanie for him. Since he never, *ever* talked about his ex-wife, Lindsey had no idea how he felt about her now.

Letting the dance steps move her a bit closer to him, she slid her hand from his shoulder to the back of his neck. It felt so good to be in his arms.

Dan lifted an eyebrow, his smile faintly teasing. ''Careful, princess. A guy could start getting the wrong ideas.''

''Or he could *finally* start getting the right ideas,'' she murmured, tightening her arm just enough that their bodies brushed together.

The song ended, and Dan set her away from him so quickly she nearly stumbled. ''Uh…thanks for the dance,'' he said.

Before she could respond, they were surrounded by acquaintances and eventually separated by the crowd. Lindsey was left to wonder if he'd gotten the message or if he'd convinced himself it was only a joke. Knowing Dan, it was probably the latter. He would find that a much more comfortable conclusion.

She knew that eventually she was going to have to openly confront him if she wanted to find out once and for all if there was even a slight possibility that they could ever be more than old friends. She not only wanted to know—she very much needed to know. She didn't want to spend the rest of her life wondering about what might have been if only she'd had the courage to take a chance.

Chapter Four

Dan had to leave the party early when a call came in about a domestic dispute that had turned violent on the other side of town. He wouldn't have responded to just any call that came in for his officers, but he knew the couple involved and feared the situation was a powder keg. Edstown was a small town with limited resources—one of the other officers was the mayor's nephew, another Dan's own cousin—so Dan helped out whenever he felt needed. That was one of the reasons he'd earned the reputation of being a workaholic.

Fortunately, Dan and two officers were able to handle the domestic problem rather quickly and without an excessive amount of trouble. That time, anyway. Because he found several more things to do when he returned to his office, it was late before he got home.

Maybe he'd just been looking for an excuse to avoid returning to the mixer, he mused, as he stuck his key into the front door of the trailer he'd lived in since his divorce.

Flipping on the overhead light in his living room, he closed the door behind him. He'd already removed his tie and jacket. He tossed them over the back of a chair as he crossed the narrow room and turned on the television. He usually kept it on just for the noise.

He fell onto the couch, pushing aside the newspaper he'd left lying there earlier. Other than that, the place was pretty neat. He wasn't home long enough to make a mess between the twice-monthly visits from the woman who cleaned for him.

Kicking off his shoes, he propped his stockinged feet on the coffee table, crossing them at the ankles. The late news was on. He tried to pay attention, but his thoughts kept wandering back to the party. Specifically to Lindsey.

She'd been joking when she'd made that crack about him finally getting the right idea. She must have been. He remembered watching her dance with Riley—standing close to him, chatting so comfortably, finishing with a kiss on the cheek. Her flirting with Dan must have been along the same lines—just harmless feminine teasing.

A man could *finally* get the right idea? That was what she'd said—as if she'd been trying to get a message to him for a while and he'd been missing it. He ran through a quick mental review of her behavior during the last few times they'd been together. She'd acted the same as always, right? Feisty. Argumentative. Exasperating. There was no reason for him to think she saw him any differently than she ever had—as a longtime friend.

She must have been teasing. But if she hadn't been…

Lindsey Gray romantically interested in him? It was a possibility he'd never even considered. After all, she was young, pretty, vibrant, smart. She had an amazing future ahead of her, wherever she chose to settle. As for him—well, he was ten years older, still smarting from a bitter, ugly divorce, contentedly settled into a predictable routine here in generally unexciting little Edstown. She wasn't the type for a curiosity-satisfying fling, so—

She must have been teasing.

Still, it was an intriguing thought, he discovered. Lindsey and him…if the possibility had ever flitted through his mind, he'd immediately suppressed it. First she'd been too young. And then he'd gotten involved with Melanie, making the incredibly stupid mistake of marrying her. When Lindsey had returned to Edstown—available and fully adult—he'd been newly divorced and admittedly bitter about it.

It had taken him this long to finally put that debacle behind him. He still wasn't sure he was ready to risk his heart on another relationship. With anyone. Especially Lindsey—who, of course, had only been teasing.

A week passed with no more fires and no particularly newsworthy events. Lindsey's reporting assignments consisted of a painfully dull city council meeting Monday evening, an equally painful junior high school talent show on Tuesday, a garden club meeting

Wednesday afternoon and an assortment of other local-interest-only events.

Whether by coincidence or his design, she saw Dan only twice. Both times he greeted her amicably, exchanged quick, meaningless small talk and then made an excuse to leave. He was obviously avoiding her. And she would never know exactly why until she asked.

When she did run into him, it had nothing to do with either of their jobs. They met in the plumbing aisle of the hardware store early Saturday afternoon.

Dan was examining a display of supplies when Lindsey turned the corner into the same aisle. She stopped a bit too abruptly, then continued toward him. "Well, hi, there. This is a surprise."

He seemed to freeze for a moment, then he turned with a smile that looked as forced as hers felt. "Following a hot hardware tip?"

"Actually, I'm here on personal business. Dripping faucet. Drives me batty at night."

"I've got a leaking pipe under my sink," he responded. "It's going to take a new joint, I guess."

"Fun way to spend a weekend, hmm?"

He shrugged. "I'd rather be fixing pipes than dealing with the McAllisters again."

The McAllisters were the couple whose latest battle had been the reason Dan left the mixer early last weekend. Lindsey knew all about it because she'd written a brief report of the incident for the weekly police-beat column. She knew Dan hated that sort of ugly scene. She wondered if the sight of battling spouses reminded him too painfully of his own unpleasant divorce.

Because it was more comfortable for her not to think about that párticular subject, she turned her attention back to the plumbing supplies. ''Have you seen the—oh, here they are.''

Dan stepped closer to examine the faucet repair kits arranged on the wall in front of her. ''Do you know what kind of faucet you have?''

''I wrote down these numbers,'' she replied, showing him the slip of notepaper she carried in her hand.

He glanced at her numbers and then again at the display. Selecting one of the repair kits hanging there, he handed it to her. ''This is the one you need.''

''Great. Thanks.''

He hesitated for a moment, then cleared his throat. ''I've got some spare time this afternoon. Why don't I come over and give you a hand with this?''

Lindsey was perfectly capable of making the repairs herself, and she opened her mouth to tell him so. So it almost surprised her when she heard herself say, instead, ''That would be great. Thanks.''

He nodded, his expression unrevealing. ''Are you going straight home from here?''

''Actually, I planned to pick up a few grocery items on the way.''

''I've got a couple more errands to run, and I need to stop by my place for my toolbox. I'll meet you at your house in about an hour and a half, if that works for you.''

''Yes, that will be fine,'' she said, studiously casual, pretending this was no different from the dozens of other times he'd dropped by her house. That, of course, had been before she'd decided to stop hiding her feelings and make a real effort to get Dan's full attention.

Just forty-five minutes later, after a quick dash through the grocery store, she stood in front of a mirror in her house, atypically obsessing about her appearance. She had donned a baby-blue spring sweater, some jeans and boots to run her errands that morning. Not grubby, she decided, but not exactly seductive, either. Of course, she would *really* look ridiculous if she put on something slinky to fix the plumbing.

She brushed her hair and touched up her makeup—very subtly, of course, thanks to Connie Peterson's expert tutelage. She debated between swingy silver earrings and big gold hoops, finally deciding on the silver. And then, deciding they looked too calculated, she took them off.

"Would you chill out?" she demanded of the harried-looking reflection in the mirror. "You're acting like an idiot."

Dan was only coming to fix her faucet, she reminded herself again. A very big-brotherly thing to do—certainly no indication that his interest in her had changed. It was unlikely that anything significant would happen between them this afternoon. So there was no need to get all bent out of shape about his impending arrival.

Maybe she should change her sweater, she thought, turning sideways in front of the mirror.

And then she covered her eyes and groaned. Maybe she should just sell the house and move away before he got there—thereby preventing another occasion for her to do something really foolish.

* * *

Toolbox in hand, Dan was just about to leave his trailer and head over to Lindsey's house when someone knocked on his front door. He groaned at the thought that it could be a summons back to work. Lindsey would probably insist on knowing all the details if he called to cancel, and if she decided there was a news story involved, she'd want to be right in the middle of it.

Maybe it was just a door-to-door evangelist or something, he thought hopefully.

Instead, he found a pretty dark-haired teenager on his front step. "Polly?" he asked his sixteen-year-old niece in surprise. "Is something wrong?"

Her bottom lip bore evidence that she'd been chewing on it as she waited for him to answer the door, and there was a somber look in her brown eyes that were so like his sister's. "I'm not sure, Uncle Dan. I found something that I think maybe you should see."

He glanced at the tattered notebook in her hand, then behind her. "Did you come alone?"

She nodded. "Mom let me use her car to do some shopping. I didn't tell her I was coming here, because I was afraid she'd get worried."

Dan didn't like the sound of that at all. He was very fond of his only niece and more than a bit overprotective when it came to his family. "Come in, Polly. Tell me what's going on."

He briefly considered calling Lindsey, but decided to wait until he heard what Polly had to say. This might not take long. Could be his niece just had some gossip to share with him about a school prank or something. She told him occasionally when she'd heard a rumor of a planned fight or vandalism or other juvenile mischief of that nature.

Closing the door behind her, he asked, ''Would you like a cola or something?''

''No, thanks. I'm supposed to meet Jenny at the shopping center pretty soon. I just thought I better show you this first.''

Because she still looked a bit nervous—which wasn't characteristic of his outgoing, gregarious niece—he kept his voice gentle. ''Show me what, honey?''

She held out the notebook she'd carried in with her. Tattered, bent and ragged, it looked as though it had been put through some hard use. ''I found this on the schoolgrounds after school yesterday afternoon. It was behind a bush, almost hidden. I think someone might have dropped it there during that big fight at lunch.''

Dan nodded. He'd heard about the melee at the school yesterday. In fact, he'd had to send an officer over to help break it up. Such things were becoming more common even in little Edstown, he thought with a sigh of regret. ''If you want the book returned to the owner, why didn't you just turn it in to the school office Monday? I'm sure it could have waited until then.''

Her expression troubled, she shook her head, making her dark hair sway around her face. ''I was going to do that. There isn't a name in it or anything, so I decided I'd just hand it in at the office in case anyone asked for it. Then, this morning, I saw it sitting on the desk in my room, and I thought I'd look through it and see if there was any clue to the owner—you know, in case he needed it before Monday?''

''And was there a clue?''

''I don't know. I didn't get all the way through it. I think you'd better look at it, Uncle Dan.''

Struck by the urgency in her voice, he took the notebook without looking at it. After a moment he glanced down, opened the book and flipped through a few pages.

The first phrase that caught his attention was ''burn it all down.'' Written in large, dark, angry-looking letters. He started turning the pages more slowly. Fire was mentioned on every page—worked into poetry, imagery, artwork, random notations. The phrase ''burn it all down'' appeared hundreds of times—printed, scribbled, drawn in elaborate graphic lettering.

''Tell me again where you found this, Polly,'' he said, slowly raising his gaze to hers.

Her expression told him she knew what he was thinking. ''It has something to do with all those arsons, doesn't it?''

''I don't know. But I'd like to know who this notebook belongs to. You said it was in the bushes behind the school?''

She nodded. ''I saw the fight, you know. All those guys started pushing and shoving, throwing things. People got knocked down, and their stuff got scattered. I'm thinking maybe this notebook slid under that bush in all the confusion. I only saw it afterward because the sun was shining on the metal binding.''

''You didn't see who dropped it?''

''No. There were only a few people still on the

grounds when Jenny and I left school. We stayed late to decorate the hallway for spirit week.''

''Did Jenny see what was written in here?''

''No. I picked it up and looked inside the cover for a name. When I didn't see one, I asked a few people if it was theirs and they all said no. So I stuck it in my backpack and told Jenny I'd take it to the office Monday. I've already told you the rest.''

''I don't want you to say anything about what you read in here to anyone, you understand?''

She nodded gravely. ''I figured you'd say that. That's why I didn't even tell Mom.''

A bit guiltily, he cleared his throat. ''We'll, uh, tell your mom later.''

His sister would chew his hide for not immediately calling her about this, of course, but Dan didn't want anyone knowing about this notebook until he'd had time to study it more closely.

Because she was as aware as Dan that her dear mother was one of the worst gossips in Edstown, Polly smiled a little and nodded. ''We'll tell her later,'' she agreed.

His answering smile faded quickly. ''I'm very serious, Polly. Don't tell anyone what you read, okay?''

She bit her lip before asking, ''Do you think I could be...well, you know...in danger or something?''

''I sincerely doubt it,'' he answered, keeping his voice reassuring. ''But just to be on the safe side, it's best to keep quiet.''

''Uncle Dan, do you think someone at my school has been setting those fires?''

He didn't want to believe that a teenager had been

responsible for so much devastation. And he *really* didn't want to believe a teenager had so far managed to outsmart him, the fire chief, and the experts from Little Rock. But he'd been doing this job long enough to accept that anything was possible. "I'll look into it," he assured her. "It's probably totally unrelated. Most likely just a kid who takes his frustrations out in writing. Like a journal or something."

Which was entirely possible, he reminded himself. But he intended to quietly show this notebook to a few teachers, see if anyone could identify the handwriting. After that...well, who knew?

"I'd better go," Polly said, looking greatly relieved to have the notebook out of her possession. "Jenny's waiting for me."

That reminded him that someone was waiting for *him,* as well. And he almost winced at the thought of what Lindsey would do if she found out about this notebook. She'd go directly into bulldog reporter mode, long before he was ready for any hint to get out about this discovery—which could very well lead nowhere.

He would just have to make damned sure he didn't let anything slip. He would fix her faucet, as he'd promised, and then get the hell out of her house and back to his investigation.

Dan was holding a toolbox when Lindsey opened the door to him just two hours after she'd left him in the hardware store. In his gray University of Central Arkansas sweatshirt and faded jeans, he could easily have passed for a sexy handyman rather than a cop.

She considered telling him so—then decided that might send him running a bit prematurely.

Play it cool, she advised herself, and moved out of the doorway. ''Come on in.''

He nodded and stepped past her. ''Where's the leaky faucet that's been driving you batty?''

''Getting right down to business, aren't you? Wouldn't you like a drink or something first? I can make a pot of coffee.''

''Go ahead. I'll have a cup after I fix the faucet.''

She led him into the kitchen, where water dripped steadily—and noisily—against the stainless steel sink. Dan set his toolbox on the counter. ''I'll have to turn the water off under the sink.''

''Oh, wait. Let me fill the coffeemaker first.'' She grabbed the glass carafe from the drip machine and moved beside him to reach for the cold-water handle. Her left arm brushed his right in the process; Dan moved back as if a static spark had arced between them.

He hadn't touched her since he'd arrived, she realized. Hadn't tried to ruffle her hair, hadn't even patted her shoulder—both gestures he often made toward her.

''It's all yours,'' she said, smiling up at him.

''What—oh, the sink.''

''Of course.'' She let her eyes widen a bit. ''What else would I have meant?''

He gave her a somewhat suspicious look, then opened his toolbox. Lindsey started making coffee. Was there really an awareness between them that hadn't been there before? Or was it only her own overactive imagination?

Twenty minutes later they sat at her table with mugs of coffee, the faucet blessedly quiet. Lindsey nodded toward the sink. "That's much better. I can't tell you how much I appreciate it."

"No need. After all, I told B.J. I'd help you out when I could."

It was all she could do not to grimace. Once again he'd relegated her to his buddy's little sister. What was it going to take to make him see her differently? She remembered Connie Peterson's advice about getting a man's attention: *Sometimes you just gotta hit 'em over the head, girl. Men just don't get subtlety.*

Short of stripping and draping herself over the table, she wasn't sure what Connie might suggest at this point.

Stalling for time, she fell back on the one topic that was always guaranteed to spark a conversation... work. "Any progress on the arson investigation?" she asked, expecting a negative reply.

The expression that flashed almost instantaneously across his face awakened all her reporter's instincts. Someone else might have missed it—but she knew Dan too well. "What?" she demanded, leaning forward.

"Nothing. You got any cookies or something? I'm hungry."

She set her coffee cup down with a thump. "You've learned something since I saw you last. What is it?"

He looked her straight in the eyes and spoke very deliberately. "All I can tell you at this point is that we still don't have a suspect."

"Then what *do* you have?"

He stood, crossed the room and opened the pantry. "Oreos. Great. Is there any more of that coffee?"

"Not for you," she snapped, jumping to her feet. "Not until you tell me what you're hiding from me."

"Don't start that refrain again, Lindsey. It gets old fast." He tossed the pack of cookies onto the table, picked up his cup and moved to the coffeemaker.

"Dan, if you've learned something that could lead to an identification of the arsonist, you really should tell me."

He sat, dug a couple of cookies from the bag and eyed her with faint amusement. "Assuming I *did* have a possible lead, why on earth do you think I'd have any obligation to discuss it with you?"

"It's called freedom of information."

"Not when it involves an ongoing investigation."

"I wouldn't jeopardize your investigation. You know very well that I would only print the information I think the public needs to know."

"Yeah, well, you and I don't often agree about what that is. When there's something concrete for you to report, you'll get an official statement from my office."

"At least tell me if you have a possible new lead. I can report that without giving any details. If nothing else, it will reassure people around here that progress is being made in the investigation."

He didn't fall for the admittedly weak enticement. "No comment," he mumbled around a mouthful of cookie.

"Off the record then." She was determined to pry something out of him just to satisfy her own rampant curiosity. "Tell me what you've got. I'll keep it to myself until you give me permission to use it."

He reached for another cookie. "No comment."

Lindsey felt her jaw drop. "You don't trust me?"

His smile might have tempted a lesser woman to hit him. As it was, Lindsey's palm itched. "Not as far as I can throw you, princess. Not when it comes to your job."

"I can't believe this!" She slapped both hands on the table and pushed herself out of her chair, beginning to pace the kitchen in a rush of temper. "I *told* you it would be off the record, promised not to breathe a word, and you still don't trust me."

He twisted a cookie and ate the cream center.

His lack of an answer only angered her more. "You really aren't going to tell me anything?"

"Nope."

"I can't believe this," she repeated.

"My long friendship with your brother—and with you—will get your faucet repaired, but it won't get you any inside information about my investigation."

That casually spoken statement literally stole her breath for a moment. When she was able to speak, it was in a clipped voice that should let him know just how infuriated she was. "I have never called upon my friendship with you to get any special favors on the job. Ever. And as for the faucet—I was perfectly capable of fixing that myself."

"So what am I doing here?" The irritation in his voice let *her* know that he was growing impatient with her haranguing him.

"If you weren't such a blind, stubborn, thick-headed male, you'd have figured that one out yourself,'' she snapped. ''Maybe you'd better go, before you decide I'm trying to buy your damned classified information with cookies and coffee.''

''Fine.'' He stood and reached for his toolbox. ''Try to do a pal a favor,'' he grumbled half beneath his breath.

''I am not your pal!''

''Look, I'll talk to you later, okay? And I promise as soon as I have any solid information to release, you'll be the first person I call.''

He still thought she was angry only because he wouldn't tell her about whatever clue he'd found in the arson investigation. ''Don't do me any favors,'' she said, more quietly now. ''Call Riley.''

Shaking his head, Dan let himself out the back door.

Lindsey thought for a moment about crying. But since throwing something seemed like a much more satisfying option, she left the kitchen before she was tempted to smash all her dishes.

She was giving up, she told herself, storming into the living room and collapsing on the couch. Waving a white flag. Throwing in the towel. Sounding ''Retreat.'' Any other metaphor for surrender that she could think of in her hurt-and anger-induced funk.

She'd been an idiot to think that a new haircut and some new makeup would make Dan see her in a different light. As for swallowing her pride and pulling that ridiculous stunt of pretending she needed him to fix her faucet—or any other chore that she was quite capable of handling herself—that hadn't worked, either. He'd just been ''helping out a pal.''

Lindsey had never easily conceded defeat—except

with Dan. She was doing so now. It was time to give up. Grow up. Move on.

Deep inside she'd always known this time would come. She just hadn't anticipated how much it would hurt to abandon her longtime dream. She couldn't just stop loving Dan, but she could—somehow—learn to stop expecting him to love her in return.

She didn't know why Dan couldn't feel about her the way she felt about him. Maybe it was because he'd known her so long and still saw her as the little girl he'd first met. Maybe he was still hurting too badly from his divorce to open himself to anyone else. Maybe he still harbored feelings for his ex-wife, no matter how badly she'd hurt him. Or maybe Lindsey just wasn't his type. She certainly bore little resemblance—physically or in any other way—to his ex. But whatever the reason, it was clear that nothing was going to change.

She just hadn't known it would hurt quite this much, she thought, rubbing her chest as if that would somehow ease the dull ache there.

Chapter Five

Dan was reading through the notebook for perhaps the tenth time when his telephone rang at nearly ten Saturday night. Well accustomed to calls at all hours, he wasn't startled by the ring. He was mentally prepared to put on his boots and head out the door when he answered.

He certainly hadn't expected to hear his niece on the other end of the line. "Uncle Dan? Something's happened."

He gripped the receiver more tightly as he sat straight up on the couch. "What's wrong, Polly? Where are you?"

"I'm at home—in my bedroom."

"Are your parents there?"

"No. They went to a movie with some friends, and I think they were going to get dessert when it was over. They said they'd be home by eleven."

The edginess of her answer had him reaching for his boots even as he asked, ''What happened to frighten you?''

''I got a phone call. It was a guy. I didn't recognize his voice. He asked if I'd found a notebook at school.''

''Look, I'm on my way over. You can tell me everything he said when I get there.''

''Okay.'' Polly didn't try to disguise her relief. ''I'll be watching for you.''

''Fifteen minutes. Don't open the door to anyone but me.''

''I won't.''

He had one boot on by the time he hung up the phone.

Apparently Polly had been quite literal in her promise to watch for him. He saw the curtains twitch when he climbed out of his car in her driveway, and she had the front door open almost before his finger touched the doorbell.

Closing the door behind him, he put an arm around her slender shoulders and led her to the deep, leather couch in the rustically furnished den. The room was decorated with his sister, Tina's, primitive art collectibles and the stuffed ducks that her husband, Ron, had bagged during the past few hunting seasons. Early middle Americana—that was the label Dan's ex-wife had given to most of their neighbors' homes. Whatever Melanie and the other decorating critics might call it, Dan liked it. He was as comfortable in this room as he was in his no-frills mobile home—a place Melanie wouldn't be caught dead in.

But he didn't know why he was wasting time thinking about his ex-wife when he had so many more important things to think about. "Tell me about the phone call."

Her hands nestled securely in his, Polly nodded, apparently choosing the right words to begin. She'd removed her makeup and pulled her hair back into a ponytail for the evening. That, combined with her Piglet T-shirt, jeans and pink-and-white-striped socks, made her look more like a little girl than the young woman who'd visited him that morning. Dan's protective instincts were on full alert.

She cleared her throat. "I was talking to Jenny on the phone, and I got a beep, so I took the other call because I thought it might be Mom—you know, checking on me or something."

"But it wasn't your mom," he offered, helping her along.

"No. It was some guy. He said, 'Is this Polly Drury?' and I said, 'Yes. Who is this?' He didn't tell me his name, he just said he'd heard I found a notebook at school yesterday and he wondered if I still had it."

"How did he find out about it?"

"I don't know. I told you, I asked several people if the notebook was theirs. Maybe someone mentioned to this guy that I'd found it. He wouldn't tell me."

Trying to suppress his displeasure that his niece had been drawn into this unpleasant case, Dan asked, "You didn't recognize his voice?"

"No. Either he was disguising it—you know, making it a lot deeper than normal—or he's someone I don't know. One of the older students, maybe."

"Exactly how did he ask about the notebook?"

She wrinkled her short nose, trying to recall the exact words. "Something like, 'I heard you found a red notebook at school. Do you still have it?'"

"And what, exactly, did you tell him?"

"I told him I turned it in to lost and found."

"That's what you said? Lost and found?"

She nodded. "I didn't want to tell him I gave it to you. I think he assumed I meant that I turned it in at the school office."

"Then what did he say?"

"There was this long pause—I thought maybe he was going to hang up—and then he asked if I'd read what was written in the notebook."

"And you answered…?"

"I told him no. I said I'd just looked inside the covers for a name and when I didn't find one, I turned it in."

"Do you think he believed you?"

"I think so. I kept my voice real casual, like it was no big deal. And then I said I had my friend on the other line, and he just hung up."

"Did you tell Jenny about the call—or about anything you saw in that notebook?"

A bit indignantly she answered, "Of course not. You told me not to tell, so I didn't."

He squeezed her hands apologetically. "Sorry, honey. I didn't mean to imply that I doubted your word."

Her sweet smile was instantly forgiving. "It's okay, Uncle Dan. I know you're in cop mode right now."

He chuckled. "Actually, I'm in overprotective-uncle mode. I'm trying to get back into cop mode."

As he'd hoped, that made her smile. It briefly occurred to him that he wished Lindsey was as easy to appease as Polly was. He didn't know how long it would take Lindsey to get over being mad at him for refusing to tell her the details of his investigation. She thought he didn't trust her. Why couldn't she, like Polly, understand that he was only doing his job the best way he knew how?

And why did he keep feeling that there was something else going on with Lindsey? Something he wasn't sure he had the courage to confront openly?

Because it seemed less complicated to deal with an out-of-control arsonist just then than a bewilderingly volatile reporter, he turned his full attention back to Polly. He took her through the entire conversation again, trying to unearth any hint about the caller's identity. But she couldn't remember anything more than she'd already told him.

They'd just reviewed the call a third time when Polly's parents rushed in, terrified that Dan's car in their driveway at that hour meant something awful had happened. Dan reassured them quickly, but then he felt obligated to tell them everything. They had a right to know their daughter had stumbled into an investigation. He warned them to keep it quiet, letting them know that Polly's safety could depend on their discretion, the most effective argument he could have used to guarantee their cooperation.

"One word about this to anyone," he added, pointing a finger sternly at his sister, "and I'll seal your mouth shut with duct tape. Got that?"

Polly giggled. Her father chuckled. Tina rolled her eyes. But no one expressed the slightest skepticism that Dan would follow through on the threat if he decided it was necessary.

If there was one place Lindsey did *not* want to be Sunday afternoon, it was a baby shower. And yet there she sat in Serena's living room, watching their very round friend Claudia Franklin open gift after gift while a surrounding crowd of women oohed and aahed at appropriate moments.

"How does Stephanie feel about getting a little brother?" someone asked the mother-to-be.

Claudia smiled and idly touched her bulging stomach. "She's excited. She says she's looking forward to helping take care of him."

Lucy Crews, a mother of four, laughed wryly. "Wait until you see how fast *that* changes."

Sitting on the couch beside Lindsey, Marjorie Schaffer turned to hand her one of the gifts that was being passed around the room for everyone to admire. "More little blankets," Serena's mother murmured. "Claudia's going to have a closet full of them."

Lindsey made appropriately appreciative noises over the soft pastel blankets, then passed them on. "It's a very nice shower," she commented to Marjorie. "I know Claudia appreciates you and Serena doing this."

"We enjoy entertaining. And besides," Marjorie added in an undertone, "I'm hoping a baby shower will give Serena and Cameron ideas."

"Honestly, Marjorie, they haven't even been married a full six months yet."

"I know." The older woman sighed wistfully. "But I can't wait to have grandchildren. And since Kara has no interest in motherhood, it's up to Serena."

"How does Serena feel about you pushing her for grandchildren?"

Marjorie managed to laugh and grimace at the same time. "I haven't said much to her about it, of course. Only an occasional hint. But fortunately I know she and Cameron want a child fairly soon, so I'll try to be patient."

They admired the next gift—a tiny sleeper and bib set—then passed it on. "How is Kara?" Lindsey asked about Marjorie's older daughter. "Have you heard from her lately?"

"Oh, she's fine. She absolutely loves living in Nashville. And her fiancé's doing very well with his singing career. He just signed his first recording contract, you know."

"I can't wait to hear Pierce singing on the radio."

"Wouldn't that be lovely? Kara's so confident he's going to be a big country star."

"Then he has a good chance. Having someone who believes in you and supports you is half the battle."

Lindsey hadn't realized how much wistfulness had crept into her voice until Marjorie searched her face and laid a hand on her arm. "Would you like to help me in the kitchen, dear? We're having punch and cake as soon as Claudia opens all her gifts."

"Sure. I'd be happy to help."

They made their way through the crowd of laughing, chattering women and into the blessed quiet of the kitchen. Marjorie opened the refrigerator door and peered in, shaking her head. ''Cameron rearranged everything in the kitchen a couple of weeks ago and neither Serena nor I have been able to find anything since.''

Lindsey smiled, thinking of her editor's occasional, almost manic bursts of energy. He said mindless activity helped him think when he needed to solve a problem or make tough decisions—both situations he had faced regularly since taking over the struggling small-town newspaper his wife's family had founded two generations earlier. Lindsey knew it hadn't been easy for Cameron to move from a reporting job in Dallas to a managing editor position in Edstown, but he seemed to be thriving on the challenge—and so was the newspaper.

''So how's it working out for you?'' she asked Marjorie. ''Living in the guest house, I mean?''

Setting covered trays on the counter, Marjorie dived into the fridge again. ''It's working out very well, actually. The arrangement gives us all privacy when we need it, and yet we're still very close—which I like. It's funny. My husband built that nice little house for my mother. Now they're both gone and I'm the aging mother-in-law living in the guest house.''

Lindsey looked up from arranging canapés to give Marjorie an affectionately chiding look. ''You're hardly an old woman.''

''Thank you, sweetie. But I'm still older than your own mother would have been, God rest her soul, so I can't help feeling quite maternal toward you. I have a feeling something's bothering you tonight, Lindsey. Is there anything you'd like to talk to me about?''

Apparently, Lindsey's emotions were visible to everyone except Dan. "I'm just a little stressed right now. Trying to decide what direction to take in my life."

"I heard you're thinking about selling your house."

"Yes. I'll be talking to a real estate agent next week."

"Did something happen yesterday to bring you to that decision?"

Lindsey was tempted to tell Marjorie the whole story, but all she said was, "Let's just say I'm finally learning to accept reality."

A burst of laughter from the other room made Marjorie glance that way before turning back to Lindsey. "Tell me, dear—have you ever tried telling Dan that you're in love with him?"

Lindsey had to swallow a couple of times before she could respond to Marjorie's wholly unexpected question. "How...?"

Marjorie gave her a softly sympathetic smile. "Your mother and I were friends. We were always amused by the obvious crush you had on Dan when you were a little girl. Your mother thought you got over it when Dan married Melanie. I wasn't so sure. And lately, well..."

Lindsey groaned and covered her cheeks with her hands. "Is it that obvious?"

"Only because I've known you so long. I happened to see you dancing with him at the mixer, and I recognized the look in your eyes. I'm sure it isn't obvious to everyone."

"It certainly isn't to Dan." Lindsey dropped her hands to her side. "He doesn't have a clue."

"Which brings me back to my question. Have you ever tried to tell him?"

"Not in so many words. But I've done everything short of that to try to get my point across. I've changed my appearance and my behavior—well, most of the time, anyway," she added, wincing as she remembered the way she'd yelled at him yesterday about not sharing his arson clues with her.

"That could be part of your frustration," Marjorie suggested. "You want him to admire you for the person you are—not someone you're pretending to be."

"You're right," Lindsey conceded after a painful moment. How would she really have felt if Dan had suddenly shown interest in her because she'd started painting her face, wearing different clothes and acting as if she needed him to take care of her? What she really wanted was for Dan to appreciate her for what she was—just the way she cared for him, flaws and all.

Running her hand through her hair, she sighed. "That's why I've decided to leave town. I need to make a fresh start. Move on."

"Dan was hurt very badly when his marriage broke up. Humiliated, as well. You can't blame him for being cautious about such things now."

"I've told myself that too many times to count. But it's been more than two years. He's had time to recover—he just hasn't met a woman who makes him want to take the plunge again," she added sadly.

"Or maybe he just needs a nudge to make him

realize that woman has been right in front of him for some time.''

''A nudge? I've done everything but hit him upside the head.''

Marjorie looked suddenly thoughtful. ''Then maybe you need a little help.''

Lindsey was definitely starting to get nervous. ''Um, Marjorie...''

Another burst of laughter announced the arrival of Serena and a couple of her friends. They came into the kitchen talking and reaching for the food, which they carried into the dining room for serving. There wasn't another chance for Lindsey and Marjorie to talk in private. Lindsey wasn't sure if she was more relieved or unnerved by that fact. There were a few more things she would have liked to discuss with Marjorie.

Dan looked up from his desk early Monday afternoon to find Lindsey standing in his office doorway. ''How did you get past Hazel?'' he asked with idle curiosity, very casually sliding the notebook he'd been reading into a desk drawer.

''She's tied up on the phone. I walked past her. She'll give me hell when she catches up to me, of course, but I'm used to that.''

Dan shrugged. ''She knows I'd escort you out if I didn't have time to talk to you.''

''But you won't.'' Without waiting for an invitation, Lindsey came into the office and took a seat on the other side of his desk. ''What's going on with Polly?''

Taken by surprise at the mention of his niece's name, he scowled. "What are you talking about?"

"There's a rumor going around that Polly's in some sort of trouble."

Dan muttered a curse, wondering how the hell Lindsey had gotten wind of this. "Where did you hear that?"

"Someone saw Polly come to your place Saturday afternoon, and then you rushed to her house later that night while her parents were out for the evening. Apparently, she was talking on the phone with her friend Jenny and she got another call that freaked her out. She brushed her friend off rather abruptly and only a few minutes later you showed up at her front door."

The pencil Dan had been holding snapped in two as his grip tightened in frustration. "Damn it. Who's been watching my niece? And how did you come by this information?"

"It's a long story."

He tossed the broken pencil on the desk and leaned back in his chair. "I suddenly have some extra time," he said, his voice grim.

Shrugging, she mimicked his pose, crossing her arms over her chest. "I stopped by the beauty shop this morning to return a book I'd borrowed from my hairstylist. While I was there, Jane Pulaski said she saw you rush into Polly's house late Saturday evening—she lives just across the street, you know. She said it wasn't long after that when Tina and Ron came home and ran inside. She said she called Tina yesterday to find out if everything was all right, and she got the distinct impression that Tina was keeping something from her."

''Maybe because it was none of her business.''

Lindsey ignored Dan's muttered comment. ''Anyway, your neighbor Mrs. Sturdivant was getting a perm, and she said she saw Polly come to your place earlier Saturday afternoon. She's Jenny's grandmother, you know, and she said Jenny worried about Polly all weekend. Jenny said Polly had been acting distracted and a bit nervous about something.''

''Hell, I don't need untrained investigators on my payroll,'' Dan grumbled. ''I might as well just talk about all my cases in the beauty parlor and let the women there ferret out the facts.''

What might have been a faint flicker of amusement crossed Lindsey's face but was gone before Dan could be sure. ''I've done a little speculation of my own. You came to my house right after Polly visited you. I guessed then that you'd learned something new about the arson investigation. As unlikely as it seems, the obvious conclusion is that Polly somehow stumbled onto a clue.''

While he had to admire her reasoning, Dan was still disgusted that his and his family's movements were so closely monitored by the local gossips. That was one drawback to small-town life—trading a certain amount of privacy for a sense of community. ''Surely you know I wouldn't confirm that even if it were true.''

''I know you wouldn't do anything that would put Polly in an awkward situation or jeopardize your investigation. I'm just wondering if there's something I can do to help stop the rumors that are going around. If I have something factual and low-key to report in this evening's paper, it could put an end to some of the wilder speculation.''

Dan might have suspected some other reporter of trying to use his feelings for his niece to manipulate him into leaking information. But, as committed to her job as he knew Lindsey to be, he was certain she would never exploit Polly for a story. Her offer to help him dispel the rumors was sincere.

''Off the record,'' he said abruptly, ''Polly found something that might be linked to the arsons. I don't want that printed in the paper yet because we've just started investigating the clue and I don't want to jump the gun.''

Lindsey studied his face for a moment in silence before asking, ''Why didn't you tell me this yesterday?''

''There wasn't any reason to tell you then,'' he answered simply. ''I didn't know that Polly's name had come up around town.''

''I see.'' She seemed to withdraw a bit more into herself, her expression completely closed to him—as it had been so often lately.

Dan wondered somberly how it could be that the longer he knew Lindsey, the more time he spent with her, the more she seemed to be a stranger to him. It was becoming harder for him to think of her as the little girl who'd tagged at his and B.J.'s heels all those years ago. That red-pigtailed urchin had been replaced by someone new—and somehow he'd missed the transformation until it had already been accomplished.

He supposed he'd been too caught up in his own life—his job, his slow-healing emotional wounds, his badly bruised pride. He'd thought of Lindsey as his pal's kid sister, his own long-time friend, his professional nemesis—but he was only now beginning to see her as a complex, mercurial, enigmatic woman.

He could even see her now as an attractive and decidedly alluring woman. Damn it.

He was dealing with a lot of emotions about her at the moment, but it seemed easiest to concentrate on the vague sense of guilt that he'd obviously hurt her feelings Saturday. "Look, no matter what I said the other day, it wasn't that I didn't trust you. I just didn't want Polly's name to come out. I didn't even tell my own sister about it until I had no other choice. So it wasn't anything against you personally—as a friend or a reporter."

"You were doing your job and protecting your niece. I wouldn't expect anything different from you."

Somehow her understanding words and her expression didn't quite match up. But he nodded, deciding not to challenge her about it.

Lindsey rose to her feet. "I won't interfere with your work any longer. I just have one more question for you—is Polly all right?"

"Polly's fine," he assured her, hearing the genuine concern in the question. "And I'll make certain she stays that way."

"I'm sure you will." With that she turned toward the doorway, apparently intending to leave without another word.

"Lindsey—" Dan spoke quickly, prompted by the inexplicable feeling that if she left now, like this, something between them would be forever changed.

"Why don't we have a burger or something this evening after work? I think we need to talk."

She froze for a moment with her back to him, so he couldn't see her face. When she turned, it was with a bland smile that could have been directed toward a total stranger. "Sorry. I have a date tonight."

"A date?" He felt his eyebrows lower a bit.

She nodded. "Let me know if there's anything I can do for Polly, okay? And of course you know to notify the newspaper if something comes through on your arson clue."

She wasn't going to volunteer details about her plans for the evening, and he wouldn't ask. None of his business, he told himself. But he couldn't help being curious about who she was going out with that evening. He knew most of the single guys her age around town—if not personally, then by reputation. He couldn't think of anyone who seemed like a good match for Lindsey. "Have a good time this evening," he said, and wished he meant it.

She nodded and left. Dan stared after her for several long moments, knowing he'd been right. Something between them had just been broken.

And it hurt.

Chapter Six

Lindsey was going to have a good time if it killed her. At least, that was what she'd been telling herself ever since she'd impulsively accepted Bo's invitation to go bowling with him.

He'd called not long after she'd arrived home from the baby shower yesterday. Her first instinct had been to politely decline. But then she remembered her resolve to move on with her life.

Going out with Bo was a first step in that direction. Not that she expected, or even wanted, anything to develop from tonight's date. But at least she was taking charge of her life again. Putting Dan and her abandoned dreams behind her.

''We should've done this a long time ago,'' Bo said, giving her one of his lopsided cowboy grins as they laced on bowling shoes.

She knew very well that Bo hadn't given her a thought in years, not until they'd run into each other at Gaylord's earlier that month, but she said only, ''I haven't bowled in ages. It'll be a miracle if I knock down a pin this evening.''

''I imagine you'll do better than that,'' he drawled, setting his boots aside and standing. ''Let me help you find a ball.''

From the choices he suggested for her, Lindsey selected a purple bowling ball, because she liked the color. Bo had brought his own, a fancy, blue-and-green swirled ball he carried in a monogrammed leather case. He had his own shoes, too. ''You bowl a lot?'' she asked, thinking the answer was obvious.

He surprised her by saying, ''Not really. My folks bought me all this stuff for Christmas a couple of years ago. I haven't bowled in months.''

''And you just suddenly had an urge to bowl again?''

Flashing her his trademark grin, he gave a little shrug. ''I couldn't think of anything else to do with you tonight,'' he admitted. ''It isn't as if there's any real excitement that goes on around this burg—at least, not very often. But I figured everyone likes to go bowling sometimes.''

She laughed. ''I don't know about everyone, but it sounds like fun to me tonight.''

''Good. That's what we're here for.''

She was spending the evening with an amusing, good-looking companion, Lindsey reminded herself. Maybe having fun tonight wouldn't kill her, after all.

Riley O'Neal was hanging around the police station when Dan left that evening. Straightening away from the desk where he'd been idly flirting with the pretty young dispatcher, Riley tagged at Dan's heels to the parking lot. "All kinds of rumors were flying around town today."

"Is that right?" Dan dug his keys out of his pocket as he approached his truck.

"Hmm. Heard you spent a few hours at the high school this morning. None of the staff there is talking about why you were there."

"They'd damned well better not be," Dan muttered. Unfortunately, none of the teachers he'd met with thus far had recognized the handwriting in the notebook, which meant there was nothing much to tell even if they wanted to talk to the reporter.

"You've obviously given the order for them to keep quiet. No one's quite brave enough to break rank."

Dan nodded in satisfaction. There wasn't much he could do if someone *did* talk, of course, but he would certainly make his displeasure known. He made sure folks around here were almost as wary of his bark as his bite. That made it a bit easier to keep order in his jurisdiction.

"I don't suppose you're going to throw me any news tidbits," Riley suggested.

"Nope."

The reporter nodded as if he'd expected that answer all along. "Okay. So you want to get something to eat? I'm starving."

It wouldn't be the first time the two bachelors had shared a meal, but Dan couldn't help being suspicious about the timing of this seemingly impulsive invitation. Was Riley hoping he would let something slip during the meal about the investigation? True, Riley wasn't as obsessive or as persistent about his career as Lindsey, but he was still a reporter, for the time being. Dan had good reason to be wary of the profession in general.

He could still picture in painful detail the headlines that had appeared in newspapers all over the state when his ex-wife had been arrested for embezzling money—along with a co-worker with whom she'd been having an affair—from a large insurance company in a neighboring town. The wire services had picked up the story of the police chief's wife who'd broken the law—and had gleefully quoted her bitter comments about her "distant, workaholic husband" and his "small-town-cop salary and mentality."

She hadn't minded using his small-town-cop's salary to make restitution to her employer and keep her faithless butt out of jail, of course.

He shook his head in self-disgust, wondering what had made those ugly memories suddenly resurface. He thought he'd been doing a better job, lately, of keeping them submerged. "Sure, Riley. Let's get something to eat. But no talking business tonight, okay?"

"Suits me. How about Kelly's?"

Kelly's was the snack bar at the local bowling alley. Dan was a bit surprised by Riley's choice, but not opposed. Kelly's was known for serving the best chili cheese fries in the area. So, okay, he'd have to eat salads for a few days. It would be worth it. "Kelly's is fine."

Even on a Monday night the bowling alley was

doing a brisk business, Dan noted when he turned into the parking lot. It wasn't as if there was much choice of entertainment in these parts.

Not for the first time, he found himself wondering where Lindsey was going for her "date" that evening. And who she was seeing.

Not that it was any of his business, of course, he reminded himself sternly. He just couldn't help being curious.

Fifteen minutes later he sat across a small booth from Riley, behind a heaping plate of chili cheese fries and a large cola. The bowling alley was noisy, of course, but it was a cheerful racket of laughter, conversation and crashing wooden pins. Dan could feel his mood lifting a little. After a long and thoroughly frustrating day, junk food and mindless relaxation was exactly what he needed.

"So how's it been going—outside of work, of course?" Riley asked around a mouthful of food.

Dan shrugged. "You know me—there's not much going on at all outside of work."

Riley shook his head in disgust. "You need a life, Dan-o."

"I tried that once—I wasn't very good at it." The remark was intended as a joke, but Dan could tell it had fallen sadly flat.

"You and Lindsey." Riley shook his head. "She was just as defensive when I told *her* she needed a life outside of work."

"You said that to Lindsey?" Dan pushed fries around on his plate with his plastic fork as he asked the question, hoping to look casual about it.

"Yeah. She's been a bit down lately. Sort of at

loose ends since her dad died a couple months ago. She told me she's getting restless for changes, which is why she's talking to Don Pettit about putting her house on the market.''

Dan hadn't realized Lindsey had already gone from thinking about selling her house to actually talking to a real estate agent. ''So the house is up for sale?''

''I assume it is. But in the meantime, she's trying to cheer herself up by changing her routine here. You know, spending less time at the paper, taking more time for herself. Seeing new people.''

''New people?'' Dan repeated, thinking about Lindsey's date that evening. Never being the type to indulge in idle gossip, he felt vaguely uncomfortable with this conversation—but it was Riley who'd brought up the subject, he reminded himself.

''Well, maybe not new—that's pretty hard to accomplish around here. But different, anyway.'' He nodded to some point behind Dan. ''Take tonight, for example.''

Dan felt an odd chill whisper down the open neck of his shirt. ''Tonight?'' he repeated, resisting a sudden impulse to look around.

''Yeah. Lindsey's over there bowling with Bo Jeffries. You know him, don't you? He's part owner of that Western supply store in Gibsonville. I did an interview with him a year or so ago about his rodeo sideline. Interesting guy.''

Dan remembered Bo. The cocky young cowboy who'd all but fallen down the front of Lindsey's dress at Gaylord's. It took all his willpower to keep from turning to see if she was wearing something equally revealing this evening. ''Did you know Lindsey was going to be here this evening?'' he asked Riley instead.

Riley glanced up from his food, an ingenuous expression on his face. ''She might have mentioned it this afternoon. That's probably what reminded me of how much I like Kelly's chili cheese fries. Why?''

Dan shrugged. ''I wouldn't want her to think I'm checking up on her or anything.''

''Why would she think that?''

''Well...you know. I'm B.J.'s friend. I've known her since she was a kid. I wouldn't want her to think of me as an overprotective older brother.''

''You think Lindsey regards you as a brother?''

Dan couldn't quite read Riley's expression. ''Maybe not as a brother. Certainly as her brother's contemporary.''

''Hmm.'' Riley stuffed his mouth with fries again.

Dan set his fork down. ''What's that supposed to mean?''

Swallowing, Riley took a drink of his cola before asking, ''What does what mean?''

''How do *you* think Lindsey thinks of me?''

Riley looked across the room again. ''I guess you'd have to ask her that.''

Which, of course, was something Dan had been carefully avoiding. Unable to resist any longer, he glanced over his shoulder.

The first thing he noticed was Lindsey laughing in a way he hadn't seen her laugh in quite a while. She looked as if she were having a wonderful time. That observation shouldn't be so disturbing to him.

His second realization was that she looked great. There was nothing overtly revealing about her outfit—a long-sleeved maroon T-shirt and khaki cargo pants—but the garments fit snugly enough to show off her slender, healthy figure.

The third thing he noticed—the one that made his frown deepen to a scowl—was that cowboy Bo was standing very close to her, one arm around her waist as he used his other to coach her in her bowling form.

''Looks like she's getting some private bowling lessons,'' Riley murmured, his tone as bland as his expression.

''It's disgusting. The guy's crawling all over her.''

''Strictly an older-brother-type observation, I take it?''

The truth was, Dan wasn't feeling particularly fraternal just then. He wasn't sure *what* he was feeling, exactly—other than a simmering urge to personally remove Bo's hands from Lindsey's derriere.

Instead, he forced himself to turn back to his food. He noticed that Riley seemed to be watching him rather closely. ''What?'' he asked curtly.

Riley grinned and plucked a dripping French fry from the pile on his plate. ''Not a thing, Chief. Not a thing.''

Dan glared down at his own half-empty plate, his appetite gone. Damn. Now he was getting indigestion.

All in all, this had been a hell of a day.

Even though she assured him it wasn't necessary, Bo walked Lindsey to her door that evening. Trying to keep it casual, she gave him a breezy smile. ''Well, I didn't bowl as badly as I thought I would, considering how long it's been.''

''Not bad at all,'' he acknowledged graciously, as

if he hadn't completely stomped her in both the games they had played.

"I had a very nice time."

"So did I. We should go out again sometime."

"Sure. We'll do that." She kept the answer deliberately vague. She really had enjoyed the evening, and wouldn't mind seeing Bo again. Someday. Maybe. But she didn't want to give him the impression that she was interested in anything more than friendship at this point.

Bo stood by while she unlocked her front door. She was relieved that he didn't seem to expect an invitation inside. Instead, he gave her a friendly kiss on the cheek, then stepped back. "See ya, Lindsey."

"See ya, Bo."

She watched him lope to his truck, and then she turned and entered her house. Her smile faded almost as soon as she closed the door behind her.

The evening had been a deliberate attempt on her part to put Dan Meadows out of her mind. Unfortunately, he had lurked at the back of her thoughts all evening, casting a definite pall over her fun. As much as she enjoyed Bo's company, she'd been all too aware all evening that he wasn't Dan. Which only proved that she still had a long way to go to get over him.

Dan met the mayor for breakfast at the Rainbow Café Tuesday morning. Marjorie Schaffer's downtown diner was a popular breakfast and lunch destination, and Dan wasn't the only one there for an early business meeting. The food was delicious, as usual, but his enjoyment of it was diminished by the mayor's very vocal displeasure that no further progress had been made on the arson investigation, despite the most recent clue.

Dan had to remind the mayor that they didn't even know for certain if the notebook *was* a clue. For all they knew it was an eccentrically artistic teenager's interpretation of the recent, much-discussed fires. The mayor didn't want to hear that, of course. He wanted this case closed. Immediately, if not sooner.

Called abruptly away by a cell phone summons, the mayor left with one last directive for Dan to keep working to identify the owner of that notebook. Dan managed not to retort that he didn't need to be told how to do his job. Tempers and patience tended to run short at times like this, and everyone needed to be careful about speaking rashly. He lingered over his coffee after the mayor left, taking the time to organize his thoughts and make plans for the day.

"The mayor looked a little testy this morning."

Dan glanced up from his coffee to give Marjorie a faint smile. "You could say that."

She slid into the seat vacated by his breakfast companion. "So how are you holding up? I know this is a stressful time for you."

"I'm fine. The real stress comes from wondering when—or if—this jerk is going to strike again."

"I know you're doing everything you can to prevent that."

As much as he appreciated her confidence, Dan wished he shared it. He knew all too well that there was little he could do to prevent the firebug from striking again unless he first figured out who it was.

"Was it ever determined for certain whether the

fire that killed poor Truman Kellogg was deliberately set?''

''No, although we're still going on the assumption that it was. There are similarities to the other fires, even though there are also significant differences.''

He could only hope again that the notebook Polly had found would eventually provide some real clues, rather than being merely a red herring. And thinking of the notebook…

''I'd better get to work,'' he said, picking up his coffee cup for one last savored sip. ''Got a long list of things to do today.''

''Of course. Oh, by the way, I'm having a little get-together this weekend here in the diner after we close Saturday. Kara and Pierce are going to be visiting for the weekend, and I want to show them off a little. Sort of a celebration for Pierce's new recording contract. Do you think you'll be able to come?''

''I'll try to drop in. It sounds like fun.''

She chuckled. ''To be honest, I have an ulterior motive in having a social gathering this weekend—besides Kara and Pierce being here, I mean. I'm going to try my hand at matchmaking.''

''Matchmaking?'' Dan said the word with the dread of a man who'd been subjected to more than his share of that particular form of torment.

Smiling serenely, she nodded. ''My friend Virginia's grandson will be in town this weekend. Remember him? Scott? The one who graduated with all those honors and went off to St. Louis to study medicine? He's a resident at Johns-Hopkins now, very close to being a full-fledged internist.''

''I remember him. He worked for you here a couple

of summers, didn't he? He spilled a whole pitcher of orange juice down my back once.'' Dan still shivered at the memory.

Marjorie laughed. ''That was his first day on the job. He was such a brilliant, serious young man, but I'm afraid he didn't have much natural talent for waiting tables.''

''And you say he's a doctor now? Scary thought.''

''I'm told he's a much better doctor than he was a waiter.''

''I would hope so. So, who are you hoping to fix him up with—especially since he's only going to be in town for a weekend visit?''

Looking rather smug, Marjorie leaned forward and lowered her voice. ''Lindsey.''

Dan nearly dropped his coffee cup. Recovering rapidly, he set the cup down very carefully. ''Lindsey Gray?''

''Of course.'' She looked quite proud of herself for the idea.

Why the hell was everyone trying to match Lindsey up with someone? ''Any particular reason you want to hook Lindsey up with a medical student from Baltimore?''

''Well, she's been wanting to make some changes in her life,'' she replied as if it made perfect sense. ''She's putting the house up for sale, dating new people. Scott's a nice young man with a good future ahead of him. And if it *did* work out, I'm sure Lindsey could find a newspaper job in Baltimore. Think of the opportunities there for her.''

''You've got her married off already to a guy she

hasn't even met yet?'' Dan had tried to speak dryly but was afraid he'd sounded cutting, instead.

''It isn't as if they're total strangers. They knew each other in high school, even though he was a class or two ahead of her.''

Dan shook his head, knowing his disapproval must be evident on his face. ''I doubt that Lindsey would appreciate being set up like this.''

''Oh, I'm not blindsiding her. I've told her Scott's going to be here. I even told her she could bring a date if she wanted. She has several young men friends, you know.''

Dan grimly pictured Lindsey snuggled up with cowboy Bo and a bowling ball. ''So she's bringing a date to a party that's being planned primarily to fix her up with another guy? And you don't think that's awkward?''

She laughed again, though Dan wasn't sure exactly what she found so amusing. ''I suppose it would be. But she said she won't be bringing a date, so that's not really an issue.''

Dan still hated the whole idea. There was just something…well, tawdry about it, he decided. Putting Lindsey on display for some hotshot young doctor to look over…she deserved better than that.

''Oh, don't look so negative, Dan. I'm not putting her up for auction. It's just a party, and she and Scott will both be there. If nothing happens between them, it's no big deal. I just thought they might enjoy seeing each other again while Scott's in town.''

Put that way, it didn't sound quite so unsavory. But he still didn't like it.

''I don't get to play matchmaker much now that

my girls are both taken.'' Marjorie sounded as if she were lamenting a favorite hobby she'd been forced to give up. ''I tried a couple of times with Riley, but he made it *very* clear he isn't interested in getting involved with anyone now. He's too busy playing and being entirely self-indulgent.''

''Yeah, well, that's Riley.''

''And as for you...''

Dan grimaced and pushed his coffee cup away, ready to bolt. ''No, thanks.''

''Oh, I know.'' She waved a dismissive hand. ''You're committed to being a crusty old bachelor. You know, I actually considered trying to fix *you* up with Lindsey for a time. But I quickly figured out that you weren't interested.''

Dan had to clear his throat before he murmured, ''I sincerely doubt that Lindsey would have been interested, either.''

Marjorie reached out to pat his clenched hand, almost as if he were a pouting child. ''Well, probably not anymore, anyway. She seems to have put her girlhood crush behind her and moved on. Which is why I've decided it's a good time to brush up on my matchmaking skills.''

Someone called Marjorie's name from across the diner, sounding a bit frantic. Marjorie sighed. ''I have *got* to hire a new employee,'' she murmured. ''Excuse me, Dan, I must get back to work. Don't forget my party Saturday evening, okay? Seven o'clock, right here.''

''I won't forget,'' Dan mumbled, though he made no promises about being there. He was still trying to process Marjorie's implication that Lindsey had once had a crush on him but had since moved on.

Okay, so he'd known she had a little crush on him when she'd been an impressionable kid and he'd been her brother's teenage friend. But he assumed she'd outgrown that when she entered high school and started dating guys her own age. She'd certainly given him no hints since then that she thought of him as anything other than an honorary big brother.

Or had she?

He remembered a few excerpts from recent conversations they'd had....

"My problem is that I've grown up, Dan Meadows," she had said. "And it seems like just about every guy in this town has finally figured that out—except for you."

And then there'd been that comment about him finally getting the right idea when he'd danced with her.

And the one at her house, when he'd asked why she'd had him over to fix her pipe when she claimed to have been perfectly capable of fixing it herself.

"If you weren't such a blind, stubborn, thick-headed male, you'd have figured that one out yourself," she had declared.

Had he really been blind? Or deliberately obtuse? Or was he even now reading things into her words that she hadn't meant at all? Had he simply let himself be unduly influenced by Marjorie's fanciful ramblings so that he was now misinterpreting perfectly innocent remarks?

He'd better get to work, he told himself, standing so abruptly he nearly knocked his chair over. As frustrating as his job had been lately, he still felt more comfortable pursuing clues than trying to figure out what had been going through Lindsey's head lately. Or trying to define his own convoluted feelings for her.

Lindsey woke with a gasp, her heart pounding, her skin flushed, her tangled nightclothes testifying to her very restless sleep. The numerals on her clock glowed red in the darkness—3:24 a.m.

''Damn.''

She shoved an unsteady hand through her hair, not at all surprised to find it damp and tangled. Her bedclothes were half on, half off the bed, and she didn't know what had become of her pillow.

She remembered the dream in painfully vivid detail.

If she'd needed any further evidence that she was turning into a neurotic, sexually frustrated bundle of nerves, that erotically detailed dream would have ended all doubt. And if she'd had any remaining hope that she'd finally managed to get over Dan, seeing his face—along with the rest of him—so clearly in the dream had evaporated it.

Why couldn't she have dreamed about playing rodeo with Bo? she asked herself in exasperation. Or getting wild and wicked with Matt Damon or Ricky Martin or Clay Walker—or one of those other unobtainable stud-muffins other healthy women her age fantasized about? Why did she have to keep experiencing these disturbing dreams of making love with Dan?

When it came to him, she was still the foolishly

infatuated, daydreaming adolescent she'd always been. She hated herself for it, but she couldn't seem to get past it. Not as long as she stayed here in this town, she told herself, swinging her legs over the side of the bed. Not as long as she could see him every day. Work with him. Talk to him. Touch him. Ache to be touched in return.

These weren't the feelings of a love-struck teenager, she thought with a low moan. These were the longings of a woman who was desperately, hopelessly in love with a man who would never see her as anything more than a good friend.

She had to get out of this town, she told herself again, burying her face in her hands. Soon.

Leaving couldn't hurt any worse than staying.

Chapter Seven

Dan opened the door of his office Thursday to find Lindsey standing on the other side, one hand raised to knock. She dropped her arm. "Oh, sorry. Hazel isn't at her desk...."

Dan masked any awkward feelings he might be experiencing about seeing Lindsey so unexpectedly behind a brusque reply. "She had a dentist appointment. And I'm on my way out."

"Are you going to see Opal Stamps?"

His left eyebrow shot upward. "How did you know that?"

"She called me. She wants me to come with you."

He sighed. "As a reporter, I take it."

Her face impassive, Lindsey nodded. "Of course."

She was dressed in working clothes—bright-blue sweater set, black slacks and boots. The garments looked new, Dan decided. As did the cool, shuttered expression in her eyes.

''What did Mrs. Stamps tell you?'' he asked as she turned and matched her steps to his, nodding to the people they passed in the hallway.

''That her son, Eddie, didn't come home from school Monday afternoon. She thought he'd gone to his father's house because she and Eddie quarreled all last weekend. But when she called there today, thinking he'd had time to cool off, she found out that he hadn't been there all week.''

''That's what she told me when she called. She was half-hysterical. I told her I'd send an officer to take the report, but she insisted I come myself. There was something else I had to finish here first, but it's only been half an hour since she called.''

''She must have called me immediately after she hung up with you. She was a little more than half-hysterical by the time I talked to her. She said you aren't taking her seriously, that you don't think Eddie is really missing. She knows about me because Eddie used to do odd jobs at the newspaper after school, and he and I always got along well. She wants me to come with you to make sure the information makes the papers. She wants Eddie's picture and description circulated so readers will help her find him if the police don't pay enough attention to the case.''

''As I explained to Mrs. Stamps, Eddie is eighteen years old. If he's decided to quit school and move out on his own, there's not much we can do about it.''

''And what if something really has happened to him?''

''Doubtful.'' Stepping out into the parking lot, he

spotted her car in one of the spaces. He motioned toward his truck. "Since we're going the same way, we might as well carpool. I'll bring you back here to your car afterward."

He read the momentary hesitation on her face before she shrugged. "Sure. Why not?"

They'd shared rides dozens of times in the past, he reminded himself. Neither of them had ever thought twice about it before.

As fond as he was of Marjorie Schaffer, he wished he'd never had that conversation with her on Tuesday. That friendly chat had planted the doubts that had haunted him ever since. Had Lindsey once harbored feelings for him? Were the changes he had sensed in her somehow related to those feelings, or was he totally off base?

Lindsey waited until they were both belted in to the truck and Dan had started the engine before asking, "Why do you think it's doubtful that anything has happened to Eddie?"

"It isn't the first time Eddie's taken off like this. Every time he gets into a quarrel with one of his parents, he runs away. We usually find him staying at a buddy's house."

"Mrs. Stamps said it's different this time. She said he's never stayed away this long without calling. She's talked to the friends he usually goes to when he's angry, and none of them knows where he is."

"Not that they're admitting, anyway."

"So you really don't think there's any reason to worry about him?"

"I'm taking his mother's report seriously. But I

expect we'll find him with one of the pals who's denying any knowledge of his whereabouts now."

"I hope you're right." She watched him drive for a few moments, then asked, "How's Polly?"

"She's fine. Not real happy to be the subject of so much speculation, of course, but the rumors seem to be dying down."

"Have you tracked the owner of the notebook she found?"

Dan very nearly let the truck swerve on the road. Tightening his fingers on the steering wheel, he demanded, "How the hell did you find out about the notebook?"

"I have my sources. I've been told that Polly found a notebook at school and asked several students if they recognized it. The next day you and she spent a lot of time together. The following Monday you went to the school, going from classroom to classroom showing something to the teachers. Some people think the notebook contained a clue to the arsons—a confession or an eyewitness report or something along that line."

Lindsey had obviously been busy chasing leads since he'd last seen her. "There was no confession in the notebook. No eyewitness account, either."

"But there was something?"

"All I can say at this time is that we don't really know if we've found anything significant."

She sighed. "You needn't sound quite so cautious. I promised you I wouldn't print anything about your investigation until you gave me official confirmation, and I won't. I don't report rumors."

"But you pay very close attention to them."

''That's part of my job,'' she answered evenly. ''Just as it's part of yours.''

Trying to ease the tension between them, he offered, ''I appreciate you being so careful about what you print.''

''That's part of doing my job well.'' The coolness of her tone let him know he hadn't made much progress in restoring harmony between them. Of course, when it came to their respective careers, they'd always butted heads. He wished he believed that was all that was going on between them now.

''Speaking of rumors,'' he said, keeping his eyes focused on the road ahead, ''I heard you've decided to put your house on the market.''

''That isn't a rumor, it's fact. I'm having a few repairs made, and then it goes on the market.''

The confirmation made his jaw tighten. But all he said was, ''That must have been a difficult decision for you.''

''It wasn't easy.'' The words were simple, but her tone spoke volumes about how hard it had been for her to decide to sell her childhood home. He wished he could understand a bit better her reasons for coming to that wrenching decision.

He wished he could be convinced the decision had nothing to do with him.

There was no more time for personal conversation, as they had reached the somewhat isolated, ramshackle house in which Opal Stamps and her son, Eddie, lived. A rusty car sat in the rutted gravel driveway. The yard was trampled down to dirt and sparse patches of winter-dead grass. Three rickety wooden steps led up to a front porch littered with broken pieces of furniture and a few flowerpots holding dead plants.

After helping Lindsey up the broken steps, Dan knocked carefully on the front door, feeling almost as if a too-firm thump would knock the flimsy sheet of wood off its hinges. The place would have been a snap for even an inexperienced burglar to break into—but there was probably little inside to tempt anyone to try to make a quick buck that way.

Opal Stamps, a fortyish woman with bitterness etched on her face and abandoned dreams hovering like ghosts in the air around her, ushered them into her home. Some effort had apparently been made at housekeeping, but the house was still cluttered and shabby. Opal directed them to sit on a lumpy couch that was covered with a faded plaid throw.

"I'm glad you came," she said, directing the comment to Lindsey. "I need you to find out what happened to my boy."

"Chief Meadows and his staff will investigate your son's absence, of course," Lindsey replied smoothly. "My job is simply to get your information out to the public."

"You make it clear that no matter what the police say, my boy wouldn't have run off like this unless something happened to him. He always goes to his dad or one of his friends when he needs a break from me, but none of them have seen him since Monday."

Trying to keep his tone patient and sympathetic, yet still reassuringly professional, Dan asked the woman to repeat the entire story, beginning with her quarrel with Eddie during the weekend.

Still directing her comments to Lindsey, who took

notes as carefully as Dan, Opal explained that the quarrel had actually been building for some time, finally coming to a head during the weekend. It seemed that Eddie had become increasingly more difficult to handle ever since his eighteenth birthday a few months ago. Skipping school. Drinking. Defying authority—both hers and her ex-husband's.

"He left here for school Monday morning without saying nothing to me," she added. "When he didn't come home, I figured he'd gone to his dad's since he'd threatened to do that all weekend. I told him to go ahead, see if he had it any better over there. I decided I'd give him a couple days to cool off and then I'd tell him to come home and see if we could work things out. So yesterday afternoon when I figured he'd be home from school, I called his father's house. Merle said he hadn't talked to Eddie since last week."

"And you believe him?"

Though Dan had asked the question, Opal kept her eyes on Lindsey when she answered. "Merle wouldn't lie to me about that, even if he'd been drinking. Even if Eddie asked him to. Merle knows I worry about my boy. He wouldn't deliberately let me suffer this way."

It was beginning to annoy Dan that the woman was obviously ignoring him, but he kept his voice cordial when he asked, "What about Eddie's friends? He's hidden out with them before."

Opal's sullen look deepened at the reminder that this wasn't the first time she'd called Dan to report her son missing. "I called every one of them," she said defiantly. "I made it real clear that I'd be calling you and that you wouldn't be pleased if you found out they were helping him waste your time.''

That threat should have accomplished some results, Dan mused. He'd had dealings with most of Eddie's friends in the past and they were well aware that he expected full cooperation when it came to his job. Even though Eddie was eighteen and could well be hiding out for reasons of his own, Opal Stamps was filing an official missing person report, and Dan would take it very seriously. The taxpayers would expect nothing less from him. ''His friends still deny any knowledge of his whereabouts?''

Opal nodded. ''In fact, they all said he's been acting strangely toward them lately. Avoiding them. Holding them at a distance.''

Dan couldn't have explained why Eddie's disappearance suddenly took on a new significance to him. Why hadn't he considered this before? Polly had found that notebook Friday, had received a strange phone call about it Saturday, and Eddie Stamps had disappeared sometime Monday. What were the odds that there was some connection between Eddie and the notebook?

He really had to stop letting himself get so distracted from his job, he thought with a sideways glance at Lindsey, who was still quietly making notes.

''Mrs. Stamps, do you mind if I take a look in Eddie's room?''

She looked a bit startled by his request. ''You think you'll find a clue about what happened to him?''

''I have to start somewhere. You're welcome to stay with me while I look around, of course.''

Twisting her fingers in her lap, Opal looked at Lindsey, as if silently seeking advice.

Lindsey gave the older woman a bracing smile. ''It's the logical place for Chief Meadows to start. Eddie could have left some hint of where he was going.''

''I've looked through everything,'' Opal confessed. ''I couldn't find nothing helpful. But y'all are welcome to look around if you think it will help.''

''Are any of Eddie's things missing?'' Dan asked as he and Lindsey followed Opal through the small house.

Without looking back at him, Opal replied, ''Not that I could tell. But he keeps clothes and stuff at his dad's house, too.''

Eddie's room was tucked into the back corner of the house, behind a door that was decorated with a battered stop sign. Dan sighed when he saw it, wondering why so many teenagers seemed to believe that highway signs were free for their decorating purposes. The room itself was surprisingly tidy, in contrast to the rest of the house, a bit Spartan but almost obsessively neat. ''Did you clean this room when you searched for clues?'' he asked Opal.

''Oh, no. Eddie cleans his own room. He's always been kind of a neat freak. Weird for a teenage boy, huh?''

''Mmm.'' Dan stepped over to a small, cheaply constructed desk pushed against one wall. It held an inexpensive desktop computer, a stack of textbooks that looked as if they'd rarely been opened, a couple of yellow wooden pencils and an empty ashtray. ''Eddie's a smoker?''

Opal scowled. ''I blame his father for that. Merle smokes three packs a day.''

''Does your son keep a journal or a diary?''

''A diary? Eddie?'' She shook her head, seemingly bemused by the question. ''No way.''

That didn't sound promising. Nearly every page of the notebook Polly had found had been filled. Wouldn't Opal have known if the boy spent that much time writing? ''What *does* Eddie do in his spare time?''

She shrugged. ''Sits behind that computer a lot, playing games and—what do you call it?—swimming the Internet?''

''Surfing,'' Lindsey murmured.

''That's it. Eddie spends most of his time in this room with the door closed. I knew it wasn't good for him, but at least I knew where he was, you know?''

So Eddie could have been in here writing in that notebook without Opal realizing it. Dan glanced at the closed drawers of the desk. ''Do you have a sample of your son's handwriting?''

''Probably in one of them drawers. You're welcome to look and see. Eddie won't like us going through his stuff, but I can't worry about that now. I need to find out where he is and make sure he's all right.''

Lindsey stepped discreetly out of the way as Dan opened the top drawer of the desk. The first thing he saw was a stack of local newspapers, the *Evening Star*. Glancing through them, he noticed that each edition featured a headline about the recent fires. His interest level immediately rose again.

Beneath the newspapers was a manila folder filled

with what appeared to be schoolwork. Handwritten papers. "I'd like to borrow this folder, if you don't mind. I promise to return it to you."

Opal studied him with a frown. "How will samples of Eddie's handwriting help you find him?"

"I'm just pursuing all possible leads. I'll also need a recent photograph of Eddie and a list of his friends, girlfriends, anyone he might have talked to about his plans."

"I'll give you anything you need to find my boy," she said fervently, seemingly satisfied that he was taking her report seriously.

Dan gave the rest of the room a perfunctory once-over, finding little of interest among Eddie's sparse belongings. Certainly nothing that pointed directly toward arson. He glanced at the computer, then decided to wait before taking that for evidence. For one thing, he was barely computer literate. He'd have to turn it over to a computer expert to find out if there was anything significant stored there—and that was best done with a warrant.

Twenty minutes later Dan and Lindsey left the worried mother's home, both assuring her that they would do everything they could within their respective jobs to help her find her son.

"You think Eddie had something to do with the fires, don't you?" Lindsey asked as soon as she and Dan were in his truck again.

He fastened his seat belt and started the engine. "I think there is some reason to speculate that Eddie might have a fascination with the fires," he replied, thinking of the stack of newspapers. "That doesn't necessarily mean he had anything to do with them."

"Did you recognize his handwriting? Was it the same as in the notebook?"

"I haven't had a chance to compare handwriting, obviously. But remember, Lindsey, there was no confession in the notebook. Only what might have been called an obsession with fire imagery. Some teenagers are preoccupied with music and poetry about death. That doesn't necessarily mean they're homicidal or suicidal."

She nodded and gazed through the windshield, apparently lost in thought. Waiting at a stop sign at a busy intersection, Dan studied her while she was looking away from him. She had a lovely profile, he couldn't help noticing. Long, thick lashes. A small, straight nose. Delicate cheekbones and a firm little chin. She held her lower lip between her teeth as she contemplated her thoughts. He frowned, thinking of the marks she would leave in her tender skin.

When she was little and hurt herself, she would come to her big brother to "kiss it and make it better," he remembered from out of the blue. Sometimes, if Dan was there, she would want him to kiss her "boo-boo," too—just to make sure it healed completely, she'd told him somberly. He'd found it amusing when she was six. Eight. Ten.

The last time he'd kissed her she'd been twenty-one. He'd brushed his lips over hers in a birthday kiss that he'd meant to be brotherly and affectionate.

He could still remember the physical jolt he'd felt when their lips had met that night. Although he'd done his best to conceal it, his reaction had been startlingly intense—and very male. Secretly shaken, he'd found himself watching her more closely for the remainder of the evening, aware for the first time that she had become a beautiful young woman.

She'd been twenty-one; he'd been ten years older. He'd felt vaguely like a dirty old man for even noticing her physical attractions. She was just a kid, he'd told himself in exasperation—B.J.'s cherished and sheltered little sister. What was he thinking?

It was only a matter of days after that night that he and Melanie had eloped. For all the wrong reasons.

Lindsey glanced his way, one eyebrow lifted in question. "You taking a nap, Chief? The intersection's clear."

It sounded so much like something the old Lindsey—his pal and sometimes nemesis—would have said, that he instinctively relaxed a little. "Sorry," he murmured, pressing the accelerator. "Guess I got distracted."

"Me, too. I've had a thought—and it could be crazy, but I might as well run it by you."

"What is it?"

"What if, instead of *setting* the fires, Eddie stumbled onto something that told him who was starting them? If he's that fascinated with the subject, maybe he was snooping around on his own."

"I suppose that's possible," Dan conceded, though he'd hate to think a punk kid had come closer to solving a series of crimes than an entire team of trained investigators. Of course, he would also hate to think that same kid had managed to commit those crimes without leaving any clues for the trained investigators to find.

"What if he did? What if something he found out put him in danger? Maybe he ran because he was scared. Or maybe worse—maybe somebody already silenced him.''

''Now you're letting your imagination run away with you,'' Dan chided. ''For all we know, Eddie's staying with a girlfriend, hiding out until his mother's willing to give him whatever he wants just so he'll come home.''

''That's another possibility,'' Lindsey acknowledged, sounding a bit reluctant to let go of her more dramatic scenario.

''So what are you going to say in your story?'' he asked, trying to keep his own voice casual.

''Only that Eddie's mother reported him missing, and that no one has heard from him since Monday. Of course, I'll probably call some of his school friends, and his father—you know, try to round out the story with some quotes.''

''You won't mention any possible connection to the arsons?''

''Of course not. How many times must I repeat that I'm an ethical journalist, not a tabloid tattlemonger? I don't know why you can't seem to get that through your thick skull.''

For some crazy reason, he was always more comfortable with Lindsey when she was calling him insulting names. He grinned at her as he parked his truck next to her car. ''I know the difference. And if you weren't so prickly and stiff-necked, you would know I wasn't trying to insult your professional integrity.''

''What are you going to do now?'' she asked after a momentary hesitation. ''About Eddie, I mean.''

"I'm going to do my job—just as you're going to do yours."

She reached for her door handle. "Then I suppose we should both get on with it."

"Lindsey—"

She glanced over her shoulder. "Yes?"

"If you want to stop by my office later today, I'll let you have a look at the notebook. Off the record, of course."

Her green eyes widened almost comically in surprise. "You'll let me see it? Why?"

Damned if he knew. "Maybe I'd like your opinion," he suggested, although he'd already had so-called experts examine the book and had others scheduled to look at it later that very afternoon.

Maybe Lindsey was as frustrated by the distance between them as he was. She accepted his offer quickly enough. "I'll be here later, then. What time?"

"It will be late before I'm free—around eight, I'm afraid. Too late?"

"Of course not. Want me to bring some sandwiches or something? You'll be hungry by then."

"Sounds good."

"Highly irregular, of course," she murmured with a shadow of her usual impish smile.

He was well aware of that. Sharing evidence with a reporter was hardly standard operating procedure. But this wasn't just any reporter, of course.

This was Lindsey.

Chapter Eight

Savory scents lingered in Dan's office even after the pizza Lindsey had brought in with her had been reduced to a grease-stained box and a few nibbled crusts. Sitting side by side behind the desk, Dan and Lindsey had pored over every page of the notebook, as well as all the papers in the manila folder Dan had borrowed from Eddie Stamps's bedroom.

"Look at the letter *a.*" Lindsey pointed to a word in the notebook and another word on one of the essay test papers. "The little crook at the top? It's very similar in both examples."

Dan looked carefully from one page to the other, for perhaps the hundredth time. "I think you're right. I tend to believe Eddie Stamps wrote both of these."

Lindsey nodded. Eddie's writing for his schoolwork was almost obsessively neatly printed. Emotionless. The writing in the notebook was very different—scrawled, splotched, angry-looking. And yet, she sensed that what they were seeing was two sides of the same person rather than two different writers.

Everything she knew about Eddie indicated that he was a young man who kept a great deal locked up inside him. He said little, participated in few school activities and had few friends, though the ones he had were very loyal to him. They thought he was "cool." Very smart, even though his grades in school were only adequate—but that, they agreed, was because he was bored by meaningless classroom work.

They all still denied knowing his whereabouts.

"Someone with this much pent-up rage and confusion could be setting fires in a twisted effort to express those emotions, couldn't he?" she mused aloud, tapping the notebook.

Dan set down the canned soda he'd been sipping. "That's what the expert from Little Rock said."

"But what about the fire that killed Truman Kellogg? If the same person set that fire, could it have been an accident that someone died in it? All the other buildings were empty when they were burned—could the arsonist have believed Kellogg's cabin was vacant, too?"

"To be honest, at this point I don't know *what* the arsonist believes," Dan confessed. "The consultants who have studied or heard about this notebook agree that it was written by someone who is seriously disturbed, very angry and about to explode, but they stop short of saying this is definitely the arsonist. As I've said before, he could just be fascinated by the fires, perhaps envious of the arsonist's boldness. We could even be dealing with a potential copycat. But there's no evidence here that indicates a calculated murder.''

He squeezed the back of his neck as he spoke, as if the muscles there were stiff and sore. Lindsey couldn't help focusing on the lines around his mouth and the faint hollows beneath his eyes. He was tired, she thought. Troubled.

She couldn't remember the last time she'd seen him look truly happy.

She tossed the paper she held onto the desk. ''You've done all you can today. You've talked to practically everyone who ever spoke to Eddie, and you've studied these papers until I'm sure you have every word memorized. And somehow you've handled all your other responsibilities at the same time.''

''That's my job,'' he said, looking uncomfortable with her comments.

''Yes. But you've put in more than your required hours today. Go home.''

''I'll go home soon,'' he answered distractedly, reaching for a file drawer in his desk at the same time. ''I just want to...''

Lindsey put her hand over his and pushed the drawer closed again. ''There are no answers in that drawer,'' she told him firmly. ''If there were, you'd have found them long ago. Go home. Get some rest.''

She kept her hand over his just to make sure he didn't try to open the drawer again. It had been a purely friendly gesture, offered out of concern for his health. How many times had she touched him in the past couple of years? Dozens? Hundreds? Yet this time...

His hand was so warm. Big. Strong. Roughened by

weather and hard work. She almost shivered, and that was just from the feel of his hand beneath hers. She couldn't help wondering how she would react to having his hands all over her.

Scenes from too many uncomfortable dreams flashed through her mind, causing her cheeks to go warm and her pulse rate to accelerate. She snatched her hand away and held it behind her, her palm still tingling as if she'd touched a live wire. She raised her gaze to Dan's face, finding him watching her with a somber expression she couldn't begin to interpret.

He'd pushed his hand through his hair so many times it looked as if he'd combed it with an egg beater. A boyish lock fell over his forehead, and she simply couldn't resist stepping closer and extending that still-tingling hand to brush it back.

"You look so tired," she murmured, wishing she had the nerve to take his face in her hands and smooth away the weary lines. But she wasn't quite brave enough for that.

How could she be so bold in her job and so timid when it came to Dan?

"Lindsey."

She realized that she'd gone still, with her fingers still threaded in his hair. Maybe she had more courage than she had realized. "Mmm?"

"What are you doing?"

"I seem to be following my impulses."

"You know that can lead you into trouble."

She found it interesting that his voice sounded suddenly huskier. "Probably."

Reaching up, he captured her hand in his, pulling it away from his hair. It surprised her when he didn't immediately release her, but sat instead with her hand clasped in his. ''Lindsey—''

She managed a weak smile when his voice trailed away. ''Am I scaring you, Dan?''

He looked down at their linked hands. ''To the toes.''

She thought about that for a moment, then smiled again. ''Well...at least you've finally figured out that you've got something to be nervous about.''

She watched him swallow before he said, ''I think we both need to get some rest.''

''Do you think exhaustion is affecting my thinking?''

Dan looked down at their entwined hands. ''Maybe it's affecting mine.''

''Then maybe I shouldn't be nagging you to rest.''

He lifted his gaze to hers again. He looked as though he were about to speak, but then seemed to change his mind—perhaps because he didn't know quite what to say. Instead, he gave her hand a light squeeze, released her and pushed his chair back so he could stand. ''It's getting late, and we both have to be at work early in the morning. You'll let me know, of course, if you come across anything that might be relevant to my investigation.''

So he'd retreated into business again. She supposed that seemed safer to him. Maybe he was no longer denying, even to himself, that she was interested in more than a professional relationship with him, but he wasn't ready to openly face that now. It was entirely possible he never would be.

But at least she could say she'd tried to let him know how she felt. She wouldn't have to live her whole life wondering what might have happened if she'd only taken a few more chances.

Maybe she'd made a little progress this time, she thought as she watched him busily straighten his desk. She could still feel the warmth of his hand around hers, could still see the expression on his face when their eyes had met and held. He was definitely becoming aware of her. What she couldn't predict was whether he would ever reciprocate the feelings she had for him—or even openly acknowledge them.

For the past few days she'd chastised herself for her cowardice when it came to her relationship with Dan. Now she was beginning to wonder which of them was really more afraid.

It should have been a beautiful night in Edstown—a full moon glowed in a starry sky, a hint of approaching spring was in the crisp air. The townspeople should have been peacefully sleeping, safe and secure in their beds.

Instead, the small-town peace was shattered once again by sirens and shouts, the roaring and crackling of a blistering fire, and the rushing and splashing of the water being used to combat it. Bleary-eyed from weariness, Dan stood to one side of the scene, feeling angry and useless as he watched the firefighters do their jobs. The arsonist had struck again, choosing as his new target an insurance sales office that had been vacated for the night, and Dan was no closer to making an arrest than he had been six months ago.

Even now his officers were canvasing the area, trying to find anyone who might have seen something useful prior to the fire starting. Unfortunately, this was a commercially zoned block filled with small businesses that had been shut down for the night. There were no restaurants or stores open late to draw after-work patrons, and this wasn't a street that led into a residential neighborhood. The arsonist had chosen his mark well—as he had from the beginning of his rampage.

Dan wasn't surprised that Lindsey had shown up. Someone must have called her—probably one of her "sources" in the fire department. Even though dawn was still a couple hours away, she looked wide awake and charged with energy, dashing from one vantage point to another while scribbling in her notebook.

Like the firefighters, Lindsey had a specific job to do—to report everything she observed and to take quotes from those involved with the action. He wished his own responsibilities were as clear cut.

"Damn it, Dan, are you going to let this jerk burn our whole town before you stop him?"

The belligerently growled question made Dan sigh and turn slowly. "Hello, Mayor."

Looking as though he'd just crawled out of bed, the mayor was rumpled and disgruntled, his glaring brown eyes bleary from lack of sleep. "Why are you just standing here?" he demanded. "Why aren't you doing anything?"

"What would you have me do?"

"Arrest someone, damn it!"

Even though he knew the reckless words were prompted by stress and desperation, Dan couldn't help responding. "Who should I arrest? An innocent bystander? The fire chief? You? I don't have probable cause to arrest anyone at this point. All I can say is that I'm actively pursuing what few leads we have, and I'm confident an arrest will be made soon. Once this fire is under control, investigators will be combing every inch of the scene. Maybe something will turn up then—''

''I don't want to hear any more *maybes.* I want some *definites,* you hear? These fires have affected nearly everyone in town. Folks are getting scared. Truman Kellogg died, and now his old friend Stan has lost his insurance company. Six others have seen empty buildings they owned burned to the ground. We've got to stop this.''

''I'll do my best,'' was all Dan could say.

''Do that.''

The frustrated public official stormed off to harass the fire chief. Squeezing the painfully tight muscles at the back of his neck, Dan stayed where he was, scanning the small crowd of gawkers that had gathered across the street. Eddie Stamps wasn't among them. Could one of these other morbidly fascinated voyeurs have been the fire starter?

Drawing a deep breath of smoke-tainted air, he started to move toward the onlookers, deciding he might as well chat with some of them, see what his hunches told him, if anything.

Maybe it was one of those hunches that made him pause just then and look over his shoulder, searching for Lindsey. Was she, too, talking to bystanders, getting impressions of their reactions? She was a damned good judge of character, with great instincts. If she hadn't chosen journalism as a career, she would have made a great cop.

He frowned when he saw that she was standing

very close to the burning building, talking to a busy hose man. No one else could have gotten away with it, of course. Other civilians were being held at a safe distance, out of everyone's way. Only Lindsey could have charged right into the thick of the action, and not only was no one yelling at her to back off, but they were managing to answer her questions without even hesitating in their jobs.

Lindsey had a way of getting what she wanted.

He was just about to turn back to the crowd of spectators when the whole side of the building where Lindsey was standing exploded outward.

Dan's paralysis must have lasted only a moment in reality, but it seemed like a lifetime. When he could move, he bolted toward the smoking pile of glass and rubble that had once been a wall. *"Lindsey!"*

Lindsey had a monster of a headache. There were other aches and pains all over her body, but the pounding in her head made those other complaints seem insignificant. It didn't help that her ears were still ringing from the explosion. And it *really* didn't help that Dan kept yelling at her.

Okay, maybe he wasn't exactly yelling at her, she amended, reaching up to touch the bandage at her right temple. Actually, he was keeping his voice low, clipped and measured. She would almost prefer yelling to this chilly composure.

She sat at the end of a hospital examining table, her bare legs dangling beneath the short hem of a thin hospital gown. Dan stood beside her, where he'd been almost the entire time since they'd brought her in an hour earlier. As soon as he'd been assured that she was going to be fine, he'd started lecturing her about being where she shouldn't have been in pursuit of her story.

"Dan?" she interrupted hopefully.

"What?"

"Could you maybe yell at me some more later? I'm a little tired."

He frowned a moment, then sighed and pushed a hand through his hair. "I'm sorry," he said stiffly. "I know you aren't up to a chewing-out right now. But, damn it, Lindsey, you scared the boots off me."

Her brief laugh was a bit shaky. "I scared my own boots off. But I'm fine, Dan. Really."

He gave her a comprehensive once-over that only made her more aware of her assorted cuts, scrapes and bruises—none of them serious, but all of them uncomfortable.

"Okay," she said before he could make the obvious comment. "I know I don't look fine. But I am."

"Yeah, well—you're just lucky. It could have been a damn sight worse."

Lindsey was all-too-painfully aware of that. It had been a near miracle that neither she nor anyone else was seriously injured when one side of the insurance building had unexpectedly exploded. Fortunately, the majority of the debris had blown toward an area where no one had been standing, with only scattered pieces flying in other directions. Lindsey and two firefighters had been knocked down by the initial force of the blast and then pelted with small pieces of glass and rubble, but the most serious injury was the hose man's broken arm. They had all been lucky, she thought again.

She shifted on the uncomfortable table. "I wish Dr. Frank would hurry and clear me to leave. I'm ready to go home."

"I wish you'd reconsider staying a few more hours for observation."

She shook her head with a force that only made the pounding worse. "I want to go home. I hate being in the hospital. But there's no need for you to hang around. I know you have a lot to do."

"I have people working on the investigation. They know how to reach me if they need me. I'll stay and take you home when Dr. Frank releases you."

He was obviously shaken by her close call, but she wasn't sure how to interpret his overreaction. She had to caution herself not to read too much into it.

Another twenty minutes passed before she was finally released to leave. She left wearing a borrowed set of green scrubs because her own clothes had been so tattered and soiled she hadn't wanted to put them back on. Her car had been left behind at the fire scene, but Dan had arranged for one of his officers to drive it to Lindsey's house. Dan took her home from the hospital in his truck.

The sun had risen by the time Lindsey wearily unlocked her front door. Every muscle in her body ached and her head still throbbed, but she was very glad to be home.

"You have those pain pills the doctor gave you?" Dan asked from behind her, closing the door.

She glanced over her shoulder. "I'll take one later."

"Take one now." He tossed his jacket over the back of the couch. "Then get into bed."

Lifting an eyebrow, she gave him a look. ''Getting a bit carried away with the bossiness, aren't you?''

Unabashed, he shrugged. ''I told Dr. Frank I would make sure you followed his orders.''

''I'm perfectly capable of following his instructions without supervision.''

''I'm sure you are. I'll get you a glass of water so you can take your pill.''

She sighed, knowing he wouldn't give up until he'd personally witnessed her swallowing the medication. It wasn't that she was especially opposed to taking the pain pill—she hurt badly enough to do so willingly—but she didn't want Dan to get in the habit of bossing her around. Treating her like a child again.

Accepting the glass of water he brought her, she swallowed the pill. ''There. Are you happy?'' she challenged him.

He caught her off guard by lifting a hand to gently touch the bandage on her forehead. ''How can you even ask me that when you look like this?''

A wave of warmth flooded through her, making her knees weaken. It was very hard to be sensible and levelheaded when he said things like that. When he looked at her that way.

He was the one who abruptly stepped back. ''Get into bed,'' he said gruffly. ''I need to make a few phone calls, then I'll be in to see if you need anything.''

''You need to get some rest yourself. You've been up almost all night.''

''I'll take a nap later. You don't mind if I use your phone, do you?''

''Of course not.'' She stifled a yawn, wondering if

exhaustion was catching up with her or if the pain-killers were already kicking in. "Help yourself to anything you want from the kitchen and lock the door behind you when you leave."

She was already on her way to her bedroom when she added that last unnecessary instruction. She had no doubt that Dan would lock up. If it were up to him, he'd probably keep her behind a fortified barricade.

She just wished she knew exactly what lay behind his tender solicitations. Friendship—or more?

Dan made a half dozen phone calls and drank two cups of coffee before he decided to check on Lindsey. He'd heard no sounds in the house since shortly after she'd gone off to bed, so he assumed she was sleeping, but he wanted to make sure she looked comfortable.

Stepping into the bedroom gave him an odd feeling. It had been years since he'd been inside that room. The early-morning sunlight filtered through her filmy curtains, providing plenty of illumination. Dan noticed immediately that the decor had changed significantly since the last time he'd visited it. The lace and ruffles were gone, as were the teddy bears, dolls and unicorn figurines—all except for the one on her dresser. The one he'd given her only weeks ago for her birthday, he thought with a frown.

Didn't she like unicorns anymore? If not, why the hell hadn't she said so?

The white French Provincial furniture from her girlhood had been replaced by what appeared to be an antique pecan set. Maybe from the early 1900s, he hazarded, though he was hardly an expert on furniture periods. She'd used deep, rich colors in fabrics and throw pillows—greens and burgundies that made the room feel warm and cozy.

Having finally procrastinated as long as he could, he turned his attention to the big bed.

Lindsey was curled in the center of the mattress, almost hidden by pillows and bedcovers. She lay on her side, one small hand resting beside her face. Her dark lashes were fanned across cheeks that were still too pale for his peace of mind, and the bandage at her temple gleamed whitely beneath strands of tousled red hair. Her full, soft lips were moist and lightly parted, her breathing slow and even.

She looked young and vulnerable lying there in her sleep—but he no longer saw her as a child. He almost wished he could. It had been a hell of a lot simpler when she was just B.J.'s little sister.

Some magnetic force drew him closer to the bed. He stood there with his hands buried deep in his pockets, his gaze focused unblinkingly on Lindsey's mouth. He didn't even try to pretend he was unaware of the urge to crawl into that bed with her. His entire body ached with the desire to do just that. He wanted her. Apparently, he'd wanted her even before he had realized it.

Acknowledging that hunger scared the stuffing out of him.

He remembered her telling him that at least he knew now that there was something to be nervous about. She'd said so right after she'd asked if she scared him—and he'd very honestly answered that she did.

He'd have to be blind and stupid not to recognize the signals she'd been sending him—and, apparently, he'd been both until quite recently. When had she decided she wanted more from him than platonic friendship? And why couldn't she see what a really bad idea it was?

He'd gone through his list of reasons so many times he could reel it off without even stopping to think now. He was a decade older than her—and sometimes felt considerably older than that. She was eager, optimistic, idealistic; he was wary, bitter and jaded. She was poised for a great future in her career, ready for opportunities she couldn't find here in Edstown; he was comfortably settled in a job he didn't want to leave. Even their careers clashed—his job required some degree of secrecy, while hers was based on unearthing as much information as possible. He was a confirmed workaholic, and she would probably—and understandably—expect quite a bit of attention in a relationship.

Even as he mentally recited the list, he knew it was mostly camouflage. The real reason he was reluctant to even consider getting involved with Lindsey was that he was terrified of hurting her—and equally terrified of being hurt again himself.

Some self-protective instinct told him a mistake with Lindsey could make the demoralizing catastrophe with Melanie seem like a minor annoyance.

Lindsey sighed in her sleep and shifted in the bed, dislodging her cozy pile of covers. She'd changed from the scrubs into a white cotton nightgown, he noted. He couldn't resist reaching out to pull the covers back over her, smoothing them carefully to her bruised chin. The back of his fingers brushed her cheek—and there was no way he could keep from noticing the velvety softness of her skin.

Again, his body reacted with painful intensity. His hand was unsteady when he drew it back and shoved it in his pocket again—not as easy a task this time since his jeans had grown considerably tighter.

While he still retained a modicum of common sense, he backed away from the bed and turned toward the door.

Chapter Nine

Lindsey woke with a low moan. It was almost as if pain had been prowling like a cat around her bed, waiting for her to wake up so it could pounce. And pounce it did—invading every muscle of her body.

She had hit the pavement hard when the force of the explosion knocked her off her feet. She had the scrapes and bruises to prove it—but at least she didn't have any serious injuries, she reminded herself bracingly.

Forcing herself to open her eyes, she focused on the bedside clock, waiting until her vision cleared so she could read the time. She was startled to see that it was after eleven. She *never* slept that late. The pain pill must have really knocked her out.

Yawning, she crawled out of the bed, muttering a curse in response to her battered body's protests. Accustomed to excellent health and fitness, she hated being incapacitated in even a minor way. Maybe a hot shower would help ease the soreness out of her muscles.

Fifteen minutes later she headed for the kitchen. She'd dressed in a loose sweatshirt and leggings, both soft and nonbinding in deference to her bruises. No makeup, and her hair was a mess, but what did it matter? There was no one to see her.

Intent on filling her empty stomach, she almost missed seeing the man sleeping on her couch.

Doing a classic double take, she stopped and stared, not quite trusting her eyesight. What was Dan doing here? She couldn't believe he'd remained here rather than going to his office. Dan *never* stayed away from the office this late!

He must have fallen asleep and lost track of the time, she decided, biting her lower lip as she moved closer to the couch to gaze down at him. He'd looked so tired lately; exhaustion must have finally caught up with him. He would be appalled when he realized what he'd done.

She hated to wake him. He looked so peaceful, and he certainly needed the rest. But she knew he'd want to be on his way quickly.

She cleared her throat and reached out a hand to touch his shoulder. "Dan?"

He made a sound that fell somewhere between a grumble and a snore. Oddly enough, she found it rather endearing.

"Dan?" she said again, leaning closer and shaking him a bit harder.

He sat up so fast they bumped heads. *"What?"* he almost yelled, clearly disoriented.

"Ouch!" she said at the same time, putting a hand to her injured forehead.

Dan reached up to catch her arms, tugging her down to sit on the couch beside him. "Are you okay?" he asked, searching her face in concern.

She smiled ruefully. "I'm fine. Another bruise, maybe, but nothing serious."

"Sorry." He touched a hand gently to her forehead, brushing his fingertips over her skin as if feeling for lumps. His eyes were still a bit glazed from sleep. "I guess I was really out of it."

"I know." Very aware of their close proximity, and the feel of his hand against her face, she spoke apologetically. "I hated to disturb you, but I thought you'd want to know how late it's getting."

He glanced at his watch. "Nearly noon. I bet you're hungry."

"Actually, I was on my way to the kitchen when I saw you."

He stifled a yawn and stretched, his arm brushing hers with the movement. "I'll fix us something. What are you in the mood for?"

Still tingling from that accidental contact, she blinked in bemusement. "Don't you need to get to your office?"

"Everyone knows how to reach me if they need me. I told them I'd be busy today, but I've been checking in regularly. By the way, I called the newspaper office and let them know what happened to you this morning. Cameron said for you to take as much time as you need, to recover."

It was too much information to process all at once. "You're taking the day off to take care of me? You called the newspaper about me?"

"Didn't I just say that? So what do you want to eat?"

She couldn't remember the last time she'd been so touched by anything. Dan never took days off. Doing so now for her, during such a critical time in his job—that had to mean something. Didn't it?

She devoutly hoped he wasn't doing these things for her only out of pity or a misplaced sense of loyalty to her brother. She wanted to believe there was more to it than that.

Which only proved, of course, that she'd made no headway at all in getting control of her feelings for him.

"Stay put," he ordered her, rising to his feet—which, she noted dazedly, were clad only in thick white socks. "Since you don't seem to have a preference, I'll make whatever I can find."

She was already scrambling to her feet. "I'll help you—"

"No." Very gently he pushed her back to the couch. "You sit. I'll cook."

"I'm really not hurt all that badly," she reminded him. "It's only a few bruises."

"Stay," he repeated, as if she were a trained poodle.

She sighed. "I'm not an invalid, Dan."

"I know. But even you have to admit you were shaken up pretty badly."

"Well—"

"Do me a favor, Lindsey. Let me take care of you.

It's the least you can do after giving me such a scare."

She couldn't help smiling. "Letting you cook for me is a way for me to apologize for scaring you?"

His hands still resting on her shoulders, he chuckled. "I'm sticking with any argument that works with you."

Because having him leaning so close to her was totally destroying her self-possession, she decided it would be wise to concede. "I'm out of bread," she said weakly.

"Then I won't make sandwiches," he replied, a bit smugly.

Lindsey only nodded.

Dan's gaze drifted down to her mouth, and his smile seemed to slide away. They froze in that position for several long, silent moments, his face hovering only inches above hers, his hands tightening on her shoulders. Either of them had only to move just a little to bring their mouths together. To send them into each other's arms.

Lindsey didn't quite have the courage to make that move. And Dan didn't seem inclined to make it himself.

He loosened his grip on her shoulders and drew away, his expression oddly grim even as he kept his tone light. "I'll let you know when it's ready," he said, stepping back.

Still not quite trusting her voice, she nodded again.

He disappeared into the kitchen and she stared at the doorway through which he had departed. What did he expect her to do now? Lie here like a helpless victim while he took over her house? Drive herself crazy trying to interpret the look that had been in his eyes as he'd bent so close to her?

Scowling, she reached for the telephone. Languishing just wasn't her style.

Riley answered his cell phone after a couple of rings. "O'Neal here."

"Riley, it's Lindsey."

"Hey, Linds. I thought you got blown up."

Obviously, he'd been assured she wasn't badly hurt, or he wouldn't have made such a sick joke. At least, she didn't think he would. With Riley, it was sometimes hard to tell.

"I was only partially blown up," she answered in the same vein. "What's going on with you?"

"I'm writing a front-page story about a beautiful, intrepid reporter who risks life and limb in pursuit of the news."

She groaned. "Please tell me that's only a joke. You're embarrassing me."

"Did I say the story was about you? It's about me."

She snorted inelegantly. "Yeah, right. What have you *really* learned today? Anything new?"

"Not much. No one saw anyone suspicious hanging around the arson scene either before or after the fire. There's been no sign of Eddie Stamps, and his mother is starting to make a lot of noise. She's getting hysterical—understandably, of course."

"Her son is missing. She has a right to be hysterical."

"Yeah. Anyway, she's claiming no one is paying attention to her boy because everyone's so focused on the arsons. And she's been asking where Chief Meadows is. All anyone is saying is that Dan's off on personal business today.''

Lindsey winced. People had to be wondering what Dan was doing taking time off only hours after another fire. As much as his friends had been urging him to take a break, no one could have expected him to do so today. She was still stunned by his decision herself.

''Dan's keeping very close tabs on his ongoing investigations,'' she said, defending him. ''But he deserves a chance to rest from the long hours he's been putting in lately.''

''Sure he does. I've been telling him that for ages. I've been saying the same thing to you, if you'll remember. So stop worrying about work and spend the rest of the day recuperating, okay? This is only your second day off in months. Lousy way to get a break, but you might as well take advantage of it. And if you're still not fully recovered by tomorrow, take another day. Believe it or not, the paper's not going to shut down if you aren't here for a couple days.''

''I know that.''

''Seriously, Lindsey, is there anything you need? I can come by later and give you a hand.''

Lindsey could hear Dan clattering pans and slamming cabinet doors in the kitchen. ''Thanks, Riley, but I'm okay. I have help.''

''Well, tell Dan I said hi. And let me know if you need me for anything.''

''I will. Thanks.''

Hanging up, she considered calling Cameron, but decided that could wait until after she'd eaten. Her curiosity was simply getting the better of her.

She stood, stretching in an attempt to relax her stiff muscles. Dr. Frank had told her it would be several days before the soreness went away, but she had no intention of giving in to the discomfort. She'd once played a tennis tournament with a stress fracture in her left ankle. She could ignore a few scrapes and contusions now.

Walking a bit stiff-legged, she entered the kitchen, pausing just inside the doorway. She wasn't sure what Dan was making, but apparently it required the use of several bowls and utensils, judging from the cluttered counters. His back to her, he worked at the stove, his cell phone wedged between his shoulder and his ear. He talked in a low voice, and she didn't try to eavesdrop, but she could tell the call was work related.

Dan was definitely still running the show from behind the scenes. She suspected he'd taken only a brief nap before she'd found him on her couch.

Dan might not be in his office, but he was still at work, she thought with an indulgent smile. She identified all too well with that sort of dedication.

She waited until he disconnected the call before asking, "Are you sure you don't need help?"

He looked over his shoulder. "It's all under control. Almost ready."

She moved toward the cupboard. "I'll set the table."

"I'll get it. You sit down."

"Dan," she said with a roll of her eyes, "if I don't start moving around, I'm going to be as stiff as an ironing board. Now get out of the way and let me set the table."

He moved. Lindsey was very careful to conceal every wince and grimace as she took plates and glasses from the cabinets and silverware from its drawer. If Dan spotted the first sign of weakness, he was likely to pick her up and carry her to the couch.

As tempting as that prospect was, she suspected it would only lead to further frustration on her part.

Dan had prepared omelets and biscuits for their brunch. Lindsey poured orange juice and filled coffee cups while he set the food and condiments on the table. They made a good team, she thought wistfully. Almost as if they'd been making breakfast together for a long time.

''This looks great,'' she said, trying to distract herself.

''I hope it tastes that way.'' He held her chair for her. ''Will you sit now?''

''Yes.'' She slid into the chair and smiled at him. ''Thank you, sir.''

Did he linger there just a bit longer than necessary? She couldn't read his face when he stepped away. She only wished he hadn't been in such a hurry to move out of reach.

To Dan's relief the food did taste as good as it looked. His phone rang twice during the meal. Both times he gave Lindsey an apologetic look, answered and dealt swiftly with the business on the other end of the line.

''I'm sorry,'' he said after disconnecting the second call. ''I really can't turn off the phone.''

''Nor would I expect you to,'' she answered

promptly. "I certainly don't mind you doing your job, Dan."

He gave a grim, humorless smile. "Melanie went ballistic every time I got a call when I was off duty. She always took it personally."

The sudden silence from the other side of the table made him abruptly aware of what he'd just said. It was the first time in two and a half years he'd mentioned his ex-wife's name. He didn't know why he'd suddenly brought her up now, but he sincerely wished he hadn't.

"Yeah, well, I'm not Melanie," Lindsey said gruffly, keeping her gaze on her plate. "Actually, I'm surprised my own phone hasn't been ringing off the hook."

He cleared his throat. Something about the sound must have implied guilt, because she looked up at him suspiciously and said, "What?"

"I turned your phone ringer off," he confessed. "Your machine's picking up calls."

She sat back in her chair and raised her eyebrows at him. "You turned off my phone?"

"I wanted you to sleep as long as you could."

Before she could say anything, he held up both hands. "I know. It was a very arrogant and high-handed thing for me to do, and I should have consulted you first."

"Actually, I was going to say thank you," she startled him by saying mildly. She reached for her coffee cup. "I needed the sleep. I'll check messages and return calls later."

He regarded her warily. "No lecture about how you're perfectly capable of taking care of yourself?"

"I am, of course. But I can accept an occasional thoughtful gesture."

"I'm glad to hear that." He finished his meal and drained his coffee cup. "I'll clean up in here while you check your messages, if you want. Don't let anyone convince you to go to work today, though. Dr. Frank said you should take a day or two to recover from the jolt you took."

"I heard him," she reminded him. At least she didn't waste her breath trying to argue with him about cleaning the kitchen. She'd probably figured out by now that she wasn't going to change his mind about taking care of her today.

From what he overheard as he cleaned the kitchen, Lindsey's calls were all from friends who had learned she'd been injured and wanted to check on her. He heard her return a few, then reset the machine. By that time he had finished the kitchen and joined her in the den.

She looked suspiciously at the glass of water he carried and the pill he held out in his other palm. "Time for your medicine," he informed her. "It's been six hours since you last had one."

"It says every six hours as needed for pain. I don't need it right now."

"Dr. Frank said you should take them every six hours today to stay ahead of the discomfort. He said it might keep you from being too sore to get around tomorrow."

"But—"

He sighed gustily and sat on the couch beside her, holding out the water and the medication. "Lindsey. Take the damned pill."

Her own sigh was just as heavy as his, but she finally accepted the pill. "I'm only letting you get away with giving me orders today because I know you're trying to be nice," she muttered. "But I'm giving you notice that I'm very close to putting an end to it, regardless of your motives."

"Message received." He watched in satisfaction as she swallowed the pill. He wondered if she'd noticed he'd made no promises that he would stop giving orders, especially if he considered them for her own good. He suspected she had noticed.

She set the empty water glass on the end table beside her. "You really shouldn't feel obligated to stay with me all day. I know you're anxious to get back to work. If I need anything, there are quite a few people who urged me to call."

He glanced at his watch, then toward the front door. And then he looked back at her, his gaze lingering on her bandaged temple. "I can hang around for a while yet—just to make sure you're okay."

Smiling gently, she lifted a hand to his face. "I'm fine," she said, speaking very slowly. "I've had a nap, a shower, a good meal and two pain pills. As touched as I am by your thoughtfulness, you have an arsonist to catch. Go do what you have to do."

The feel of her soft hand against his face broke something loose inside him. He caught her fingers in his and pulled her hand around to his mouth. He dropped a kiss in her palm, then closed her fingers around it, keeping her folded hand in his. "When I saw that wall explode around you this morning—"

He had to stop to clear his throat. "It really shook me," he said finally, frustrated by the massive understatement. He could still picture that wall toppling, Lindsey going down, debris raining on her—and himself not able to even move to find out if she was all right. That moment of inaction—so unlike his usual quick responses—still loomed in his memory, seeming so much longer than real time had been. For the first time in his life he had understood the term *paralyzed by fear.*

"I didn't mean to give you such a scare. If I'd had any idea anything like that could happen, I wouldn't have been so close, I assure you."

"Maybe next time you'll use better judgment," he growled.

"Now don't spoil everything with another lecture. You were being so sweet."

That made him frown. "I'm not sweet."

"Not under normal circumstances," she agreed amiably. "But you have been today. Even if it's only because you care enough to worry about me, I appreciate it."

"Of course I care," he muttered, keeping his eyes on their clasped hands. "Hell, Lindsey, I've known you most of your life. The better part of mine, for that matter."

Sitting very still, she hesitated a moment before asking, "Is that all there is between us, Dan? A long-time friendship?"

He considered his own words carefully before replying, "A very special friendship."

She scooted just a bit closer to him, so that their thighs brushed. "How special?"

His whole body reacted to that light contact. "Lindsey…" His voice was gruff.

She wrinkled her nose—an expression that only made him want to kiss her more. ''You always say my name in just that tone when I begin to make you nervous.''

''Sweetheart, lately you keep me shaking in my boots all the time,'' he said ruefully.

The unguarded endearment brought a smile to her lips. ''I've been told that it sometimes takes a figurative blow to the head to get some men's attention. I was beginning to think I was going to have to resort to a two-by-four with you.''

Oh, she had his attention, all right. He couldn't pinpoint the exact moment she'd claimed it, but he'd hardly stopped thinking about her for the past three weeks. Even when he'd been fully occupied with other matters, thoughts of Lindsey had hovered at the back of his mind, waiting to reclaim his attention.

Despite all the times he had advised himself to resist his feelings for her, to discourage her attentions for her own good, all it took was for her to wrinkle her nose and smile at him—or to touch his face—and his willpower crumbled.

No, he couldn't say when he'd first decided he wanted Lindsey Gray, but he was quite sure the wanting had only grown stronger since that point.

''Lindsey,'' he began again, not certain what he meant to say afterward. His phone cut him off before he had a chance to decide.

He sighed and released Lindsey's hand so he could retrieve the phone from his shirt pocket. ''I'm sorry.''

She shook her head. ''You have work to do. Answer your call.''

Even as he spoke into the palm-size phone, he was

struck again by how understanding she was about the demands of his job. He didn't know how long her patience would hold out if they got more involved. As reluctant as he was to compare Lindsey to his ex-wife, he couldn't help remembering how deeply Melanie had come to resent his job.

He enjoyed his work—but, more than that, he felt obligated to it. It wasn't a predictable, nine-to-five, five-days-a-week career: lawbreakers didn't exactly keep banker's hours. The chief of police of a small, understaffed city didn't have the luxury of making plans well in advance or expecting uninterrupted evenings or weekends. Sure, it was basically a quiet town with few crimes on the whole, giving him quite a bit of free time under normal circumstances, but neither he nor anyone else could predict when those circumstances would change—like now, with this unprecedented string of arsons.

"I'll be there as soon as I can," he said in response to the urgent request on the other end of the line, and disconnected the call to look at Lindsey. He watched her face as he said, "It looks like I'm going to have to leave for a little while."

There wasn't a trace of disapproval in her expression when she nodded and replied, "I understand. Can you tell me what's going on?"

"Nothing new," he assured her. "I just need to make an appearance, I think."

It was true, of course. He did feel the need to check in at work, especially at such a stressful time for his staff. But maybe he was also running—retreating again from a potentially explosive exchange with Lindsey.

Glancing at the bandage on her temple, he felt like a heel for letting his cowardice reverse his resolve to take the day off and help her out today. ''You're sure you'll be okay on your own for a little while? Maybe I should call someone to come sit with you—I bet Marjorie Schaffer would come. The diner's closed by now.''

''Marjorie has other things to do, and I don't need a baby-sitter,'' Lindsey argued mildly. ''I'll be fine, Dan. Actually, that pain pill is making me a little sleepy. I'll probably take a nap.''

''But—''

''If I need anything, I know your cell number,'' she reminded him. ''You'd come running if I called, wouldn't you?''

''Of course.''

''There you are, then. Go earn your salary and keep the mayor happy. And let me know if there are any new developments in either the arsons or Eddie Stamps's disappearance, will you?''

''Sure.'' Reluctantly, he stood. ''You'll call if you need me? Promise?''

''Cross my heart.''

He was finding it surprisingly hard to leave her. ''Do you need anything before I go? Some juice? Something else to eat?''

''I'm fine. Go.''

He leaned over, intending to brush a kiss across her bruised forehead. A nice, platonic, friendly, sympathetic gesture, he told himself. He didn't know if she just happened to tilt her head at the right moment or if maybe his own aim was the culprit, but the kiss landed on her lips instead.

And lingered.

For a first real kiss in more than five years, it felt amazingly familiar. Their lips met smoothly, without awkwardness or fumbling, and the sense of sheer rightness was almost overwhelming. As was the rush of hunger that swiftly followed.

Her arms went up and around his neck. She tightened them just a little, as if to pull him down to her—and he almost went along. He could have had her beneath him easily enough, her body sinking into the soft cushions of the couch, his covering her…and, oh, man, did he want that…but he had work to do. At least, that made a safe, convenient excuse.

He still wasn't convinced that being with Lindsey was wise—and he still didn't know which of them was most in danger of being hurt if they tried and failed. But he was beginning to wonder if they had gone too far now to go back to the way things had been before.

He pulled away slowly. "I'll be back later to check on you."

"There's a key in the flowerpot on the right side of the door if I'm asleep when you come back," she said, her gaze locked with his.

He cleared his throat. "We'll talk about the recklessness of that hiding place when I return."

"We can talk about whatever you want," she murmured, a look of invitation in her brilliant green eyes that almost had him making a dive for the couch again.

He turned and marched out the door before he could change his mind and do something that could never be reversed.

Chapter Ten

Lindsey was sleeping when Dan returned. Drugged by the pain pill she hadn't wanted to take, she'd fallen asleep on the couch watching cable news. She didn't know how long she'd been out of it, but she opened her eyes to find Dan sitting in a chair nearby, watching her.

Lying curled on her side, one cheek cushioned by a throw pillow, she gazed back at him without sitting up. "You weren't gone long."

"Longer than you think. You've probably been asleep for most of the afternoon."

"It's those pills," she grumbled. "They knock me out. I don't want to take any more of them."

"You aren't in any pain?"

Still without moving, she took a mental inventory. "My head hurts a little, I've got some sore muscles and a few throbbing bruises, and my mouth is so dry it feels dusty, but other than that, I've got no complaints.''

''I'll get you a glass of water,'' he said, standing.

She thought about sitting up while he was gone, but it seemed like too much effort just then. Her grandmother's afghan was draped over her shoulders; she snuggled a bit more comfortably beneath it and let her eyelids close again. She wasn't really sleepy now, just still drifting on a medication cloud. She rarely took pills of any sort, and when she did, she usually reacted strongly. She'd joked that ordinary aspirin could knock her out for hours.

She felt Dan's hand brush her hair back from her face, his touch tender over the bulky bandage. ''Are you going back to sleep?''

''No.'' She moved against his hand like a sleepy cat. ''Just taking my time waking up.''

''You want this water?''

That offer gave her the incentive to open her eyes and push herself upright, with the help of a hand from Dan. He'd put ice in the water, and it tasted cool and wonderful. She drained the glass.

''I needed that,'' she said, setting the empty tumbler on the end table and smiling at him. ''Thank you.''

''You're welcome.''

She patted the couch beside her, wondering what the odds were that he would give her another one of the amazing kisses. ''Sit down?''

He glanced at the couch, and then at the chair in which he'd been sitting earlier. She cleared her throat and patted the couch again.

Though he shot her a somewhat wary frown, he sat, perched almost on the edge of the couch.

Obviously he needed to relax a bit. And the best way to put Chief Dan Meadows at ease was to get him talking about work. ''Tell me about the investigations. Has anything new come up?''

''Are you asking as a reporter or as an interested citizen?''

''I'm asking as Lindsey.''

''Oh, in that case...'' He gave her a little smile. ''None of your business.''

Feigning outrage, she punched his arm.

He laughed and rubbed his bicep. ''Okay. I'm kidding. But really, there's very little new to tell you. There was a report that Eddie Stamps was spotted in Little Rock yesterday, but we haven't been able to confirm that. The arson inspectors found a couple of leads today—maybe there's something traceable.''

She lifted her eyebrows at that. ''Really? Like what?''

''I'll let you know as soon as I get an official report.''

An annoying answer, but typical of Dan. He wasn't going to suddenly turn chatty and expansive just because they'd kissed. And speaking of that kiss...

She oh-so-casually scooted a bit closer to him. ''What else did you do while you were gone?''

He stretched to reach for the remote to turn down the television, the seemingly idle motion inching him a bit farther away from her. ''Not much. Returned some calls, signed off on some paperwork, met for a few minutes with Mrs. Stamps.''

''How's she holding up?''

"Not very well, as you can imagine. She wants answers about her son."

"What about the boy's father? Have you heard from him?"

"Merle's on a drinking binge, I'm afraid. He's not saying much of anything. Whether the bender started before his son's disappearance or because of it, I couldn't say."

"You still have no evidence to suggest that Eddie's met with foul play?"

"None. As I mentioned, one of his schoolmates thought he spotted Eddie at a teen club in Little Rock, but he said he never got close enough to be certain."

Somehow, Dan had ended up almost pressed against the arm of the couch, with Lindsey still right beside him. He literally had nowhere else to go. As if he'd abruptly become aware of their changing positions, he frowned down at her. "Why do I have this sudden sensation that I'm being stalked like a twelve-point buck in deer season?"

"And why do *I* suddenly feel like an amorous teenage boy trying to get to second base with his skittish date?"

Dan smiled a bit nervously in response to her teasing. "I'm trying to be sensible here."

"Why?"

He blinked. "Because someone has to be."

She rested a hand on his thigh, feeling the muscles tense beneath the denim. "Why?"

"Lindsey—"

Because he had said her name in just that tone again, she giggled, feeling deliciously bold. Maybe it was the bump on her head that was causing her to act so out of character with Dan—or maybe it was just time for her to fish or cut bait, as her father would have said. Whatever the catalyst, she had Dan's full attention now. She would hate to waste yet another opportunity to find out if there was any chance of a future for them together.

Dan's expression suddenly turned serious. "We need to slow this down."

"Slow down?" She sighed gustily. "Dan, we've known each other for twenty years! How much more time do you think we need?"

He looked vaguely sheepish, but stubbornly persisted with his argument. "We've known each other as friends. Professional associates, in some ways. It's only very recently there's been any hint of anything else."

"It's only very recently you've started noticing those hints," she amended. "And, correct me if I'm wrong—you don't seem to be trying too hard to escape."

"You aren't wrong," he conceded after a very long moment, making her pulse speed up again. "I'd be lying if I said I wasn't interested. I just want to be…careful."

He was interested. That was exactly what she'd wanted to hear. "Okay. So, now what?"

Again, her directness seemed to take him aback. "Well…uh…"

"I need some guidelines here, Dan. Are we going to try dating? See each other discreetly in private until we want to go public? Keep pretending we're just friends while you think about this some more?"

He scowled. "Hell, Lindsey, I don't know."

"Sorry if I'm making you uncomfortable, but I like things spelled out. Straightforward. Out in the open."

His mouth twisted ruefully. "No kidding, hotshot reporter."

"I'm not talking about my work."

"No, but you could be. Your passion for getting everything out in the open is what led you into journalism in the first place."

"Probably. But anyway, what I'm saying is—"

The ringing of a telephone cut through her words. Dan reached automatically for his shirt pocket. Lindsey smiled and shook her head. "That's mine. I turned the ringers back on after you left."

The phone was on the end table beside Dan. She had to stretch over him to reach it. She deliberately took her time doing so. She was rewarded by a sound from Dan that might have been a low groan.

Oh, yeah, she thought, picking up the receiver. She was getting to him. "Hello?"

"Lindsey? Hi, it's Bo. I heard you were hurt. Are you okay?"

"Why, Bo, how nice of you to call. I'm fine, thanks. Just a little bruised."

She felt Dan stiffen against her even as Bo replied, "The word is going around that you were involved in an explosion while you were covering the latest arson fire."

"Yes, I was—but fortunately, the injuries were minor."

"I'm glad to hear that. Any news about the arson investigation? Are the cops any closer to solving the case than they were before?"

''Not as far as I know,'' she answered circumspectly.

''Guess I'll have to keep reading the papers to find out more, huh? So—is there anything I can do for you? I can bring takeout by your house this evening.''

''Thank you, Bo, but I'm getting lots of help.''

''Okay, well—you give a holler if you need anything, you hear?''

''I'll do that.''

They ended the call on that friendly note. Lindsey hung up her phone, then glanced at Dan, who was scowling rather fiercely. Still leaning against him, she murmured, ''That was Bo.''

''So I gathered.''

''He heard I was hurt and called to check on me.''

''Big of him.''

''He was just being nice, Dan.''

''Did he ask you out again?''

That blunt question made her eyebrows rise. ''Again?''

''I know you had a date with him earlier this week.''

''Been listening to gossip, Chief?'' She knew *she* hadn't told him who she'd been out with Monday night.

''Actually, I saw you with him.'' Dan looked briefly uncomfortable. ''Riley and I had dinner at Kelly's Monday night.''

Lindsey was taken aback that Dan had been so close to her without her knowledge. It made her uncomfortable to think of him watching her on a date with another man. Not that anything had happened during that date except some bowling and laughter, but still…

"I went out with him because you made me mad," she confessed.

"You went out with him to spite me?"

"To move on from you," she corrected him.

That silenced him for a moment. He looked down at her hand, which still rested on his thigh. "That's probably the smartest thing for you to do," he said after a while.

She swallowed before asking, "Is that what you want me to do?"

He covered her hand with his. "No. Damn it."

The grudging mutter startled another quick laugh from her. "Try to restrain your enthusiasm, will you, Chief?"

"I've *been* trying to restrain myself," he answered, reaching for her. "It isn't working."

Tumbling into his arms, she lifted her face to his. "I'm very glad to hear that," she murmured just before his mouth covered hers.

There was nothing platonic or fraternal about this embrace. Dan kissed her in a way that left no further doubt that he saw her as a grown woman—and a desirable one, at that. She could tell he was taking care with her bruises, but that was the only way in which he held back.

The kiss thrilled her to her toes.

Oblivious to whatever aches and pains lingered from her mishap, she threw her arms around him and returned the kiss with all the enthusiasm she'd been holding back for so very long. There might have been twinges of physical discomfort, but they were far overshadowed by pleasure. As many times as she had fantasized about kissing Dan, reality was even better than imagination.

A small shift on his part had her sitting in his lap, her arms locked around his neck, his hands sliding down her back in a preliminary foray of exploration. She almost purred.

His mouth was firm, warm, so very clever. He kissed her deeply, softly. And then he tilted his head to try a different angle, this time more firmly.

She could have happily kept trying variations of that kiss for hours.

And then Dan's phone buzzed.

Both of them groaned simultaneously. Reluctantly releasing her mouth, Dan rested his forehead against hers. ''I'm sorry.''

''I've known all along that this came with the territory.'' She wanted to make it very clear that she was no Melanie, competing with his job for his attention. ''Answer your call.''

He did, and it took her only a moment to realize from his tone that he was going to have to leave again. The hardness of his lap beneath her was ample proof that he would like to stay; she somewhat wistfully told herself she should be content with that. At least she knew now that he did want her.

That was a good deal further along than they'd been yesterday.

''I have to go,'' he said when he disconnected, confirming what she'd already guessed. ''I can't say how long I'll be gone this time.''

''There's really no need for you to come back this evening,'' she assured him. ''I'm perfectly all right.

I've got plenty to eat and pain pills if I need them—which I don't think I will. You do what you have to do—and, yes, I'll call if I need you,'' she added, anticipating his next words.

He hesitated, then nodded. ''I'll call you later.''

''Do that. I'll be curious about what's going on.''

He brushed a kiss over the end of her nose and set her off his lap. ''When are you *not* curious?''

She stood and followed him to the door. As reluctant as she was to see him leave, she decided it wasn't such a bad thing to spend a few hours apart now. She wanted to think about some of the things they'd said—well, actually, he hadn't said much; she needed to think about what *that* meant, too. They had plenty of time now. There was no need to ruin everything by rushing.

''I'm sure Marjorie invited you to her party at the diner tomorrow evening,'' Dan said at the door.

''Of course. She's very excited about it. Are you going?''

''Probably—unless something comes up, of course.''

''Marjorie understands about the demands of your job.''

He stood still for a moment, one hand on the doorknob, then suddenly blurted, ''So you're planning to be there? If you're up to it, I mean?''

She was finding it very interesting that this man who was so firm and decisive in every other aspect of his life was displaying such awkward hesitation when it came to their evolving relationship. ''I'll be there.''

For a moment she thought he might suggest they

go together. A date—a first real, public date. Maybe he'd intended to ask, but changed his mind. Or got cold feet. All he actually said was, "I'll see you there."

"All right." *Don't push him, Lindsey.*

There was plenty of time—now that they had taken that first, tentative step forward.

Judging from the crowd in the Rainbow Café Saturday evening, Marjorie's casual reception for her daughter and her fiancé was quite a success. Festively decorated with balloons and sparkling cardboard-and-glitter music notes hanging from the ceiling, and a large banner congratulating Pierce Vanness on his new record deal, the diner was crowded with chattering friends and well-wishers.

"Look at Lindsey, will you?" Riley O'Neal shook his head in indulgent amusement as he spoke to Dan. "She's eating up all this attention."

Standing on one side of the diner with a glass of Marjorie's fruit punch in one hand, Dan didn't need Riley to point in Lindsey's direction. He'd already been watching her.

From the time he'd arrived at the diner half an hour earlier, Lindsey had been completely surrounded. Everyone there had heard about the explosion, of course, and they wanted all the juicy details. He was relieved to see that the color had returned to her face, and her eyes were bright and clear again. She still wore the neat white bandage at her temple, but she'd covered most of her bruises with makeup and a long-sleeved, brightly striped sweater that was short enough to reveal just a glimpse of firm midriff above her jeans when she moved.

She looked great. And he wasn't the only man who noticed, he realized, scowling toward Virginia Porter's grandson, Dr. Scott McAdoo, who was chatting animatedly with Lindsey at that very moment. The doctor seemed quite taken.

Dan was half-seriously considering arresting the guy for something when Riley spoke again. ''Marjorie looks pleased that Lindsey and the handsome young doctor are getting along so well,'' he murmured, his attention wandering to their hostess. ''She's matchmaking again, obviously.''

''Apparently.''

Riley shuddered dramatically. ''Have you ever had her turn her matchmaking instincts in your direction? It's terrifying.''

Remembering Marjorie's comment that she'd once considered trying to fix him up with Lindsey, Dan shook his head. ''She's never tried with me.''

''You're lucky. I had to speak very firmly with her to get her to lay off. Every once in a while I still catch that gleam in her eyes.''

Dan was still looking at Lindsey, who was laughing at something Scott had said. What was she doing flirting with another guy only hours after telling Dan she was interested in *him?*

Of course, he and Lindsey weren't attending this event as a couple. Trying to avoid drawing public speculation their way, Dan had hardly even spoken to her since they'd arrived. Surely she understood why he was being so circumspect; she knew how gossip flew around this town—especially when it concerned him.

Maybe she *did* understand, and her apparent interest in Scott was merely a smoke screen.

Or maybe not. He studied the young doctor with an attempt at dispassion. He could see why a woman would be attracted to the guy. Scott was good-looking, in a clean-cut, male-model sort of way. He had a stellar future ahead of him in medicine. He was basically just getting started in life, on the fast track to success.

Damn it, *he* should be pushing Lindsey into the guy's arms—for her own good.

Lindsey chose that moment to look his way and send him a smile that made his heart stop—and then resume again at roughly twice the speed. He saw now that it was an entirely different smile than the ones she'd been giving Scott. If this smile was as readable to everyone else as it was to him, all their efforts at discretion had been wasted.

''Excuse me,'' he said abruptly to Riley, and made his way across the room to Lindsey's side.

Lindsey greeted him by catching his left hand and pulling him closer to her—a seemingly casual gesture made more intimate by a warm squeeze of fingers. ''Dan, you've met Dr. McAdoo, haven't you?''

''Yes, Marjorie introduced us earlier.'' The two men nodded cordially, but Dan sensed that Scott was sizing him up and wondering about his relationship with Lindsey. Apparently Dan wasn't the only one who had noticed nuances in the smile she'd given him.

The room seemed suddenly too small. Too crowded.

The music and laughter were too loud. And too many people seemed to be staring at them.

"I'm sorry to interrupt your conversation," he said, making an abrupt decision. "I didn't want to leave without saying goodbye."

"You're leaving?" Lindsey looked more curious than surprised. "Did you get a call?"

"I, uh, have some things to do."

She smiled wryly. "In other words, you've had all the socializing you can take and you'd rather be working."

He searched her expression for any sign of mockery or criticism, but found only gentle understanding. But he didn't know whether to trust his interpretation—or the longevity of her patience.

Dan took his leave of Scott, then turned toward the door, resisting his reluctance to leave Lindsey there with the other guy.

Marjorie caught him before he reached the door. "Surely you aren't leaving already. Pierce is going to sing for us."

"I'm sorry to miss that, but I have some calls to make this evening concerning the arson investigation. And I want to follow up on the one slim lead we have in the Eddie Stamps case—his possible sighting in Little Rock. I've faxed a photo of him to a friend in the LRPD and he was going to do some checking around for me this evening."

As he'd expected, Marjorie's concern for the missing teenager outweighed her desire to keep Dan at her party. "Oh, I hope they find him. Poor Opal is worrying herself sick."

"We're doing all we can."

"I know you are." She smiled and patted his arm. "Thank you for stopping by, Dan. It's always good to see you."

On an impulse, he brushed a kiss across her softly lined cheek. "Good night, Marjorie."

He glanced over his shoulder as he stepped out into the quiet parking lot—and saw Marjorie watching him with an expression that made him wonder what well-intentioned schemes were forming in her mind now. Remembering Riley's comments about the dear lady's matchmaking instincts, Dan sincerely hoped she wasn't considering him as her next victim. His social life was complicated enough at the moment.

Chapter Eleven

Dan didn't go to his office when he left the diner. Instead he went home, making calls and doing paperwork from there. Because it was too quiet in his mobile home, he turned on the radio to a classic rock station. Maybe by concentrating on his work and the music, he wouldn't have a chance to dwell on memories of Lindsey smiling up at handsome Dr. McAdoo.

It was just after 9:00 p.m. when someone knocked on his front door. Remembering that his last unexpected visitor had been his niece, he hurried to answer, hoping Polly hadn't stumbled into further trouble.

His caller wasn't Polly.

Giving him a breezy smile that didn't quite match the expression in her eyes, Lindsey held out a paper plate covered with a paper napkin. ''You left before Marjorie brought out the food. I brought you some treats.''

He was well aware that the snacks weren't the reason she had come to him. He wondered how much courage it had taken for her to make the overture. He wasn't even sure he had enough to take her up on it.

He saw the faintest flicker of uncertainty cross her face—as if she'd read the doubt in his expression. And he knew he wouldn't be turning her away. ''Come in,'' he said, moving out of the doorway.

She seemed to square her shoulders before she complied. Coming to a stop in the living room, she glanced around with open curiosity, making Dan realize that she hadn't visited him here since shortly after he'd moved in nearly two and a half years earlier.

Trying to see the place through her eyes, he almost grimaced. He hadn't done much in the way of decorating. The furniture was plain and functional, and the walls were bare of decoration. A state-of-the-art computer system rested on a desk in one corner of the room, next to a small, overflowing bookcase. The place looked more like a temporary office than a home. Maybe because that was the way he tended to think about it.

He looked at her again. She still wore the skimpy, jewel-toned striped sweater and low-slung, boot-cut jeans she'd worn to the party. As far as he was concerned, this outfit was every bit as alluring as the sexy green dress she'd worn to the March Mixer or the even more blatantly seductive black dress she'd had on that night at Gaylord's.

He realized abruptly that she was still holding the plate of snacks from the party. "Here, let me take that."

He set the plate on the coffee table and then stuck his hands in his pockets because he didn't know what else to do with them. "I just made a fresh pot of coffee. Decaf. Would you like a cup?"

She sat on the couch and draped an arm across the back. "Coffee sounds good."

It was obvious that she was in no hurry to leave. She looked completely at ease reclining so comfortably on his couch; he wondered just how difficult it was for her to maintain that casual pose. He couldn't seem to manage it, himself.

It only took a few minutes to fetch two mugs of coffee from his tiny, rarely used kitchen. He knew how Lindsey drank hers—with just a touch of milk—so he didn't bother asking. Setting both cups on the coffee table, he sat next to her on the couch. "What did you bring?" he asked, lifting the paper napkin from the plate she'd brought—a blatant delaying tactic.

"A stack of those pecan fudge balls you like so much."

He smiled in anticipation. "No one makes these better than Marjorie. Do you want one?"

"Thanks, but I ate way too many of them before I left the party."

He popped a candy into his mouth, savoring the taste. He'd always had a predilection for chocolate. He was just starting to acknowledge an even more compelling weakness for Lindsey.

She watched him over the rim of her mug as she

sipped her coffee. He held his own mug cradled loosely in his hands, searching his mind for something innocuous to say. Nothing came to him right offhand. Lindsey set her mug on the table, then picked up another piece of fudge. ''You aren't going to stop with just one, are you?''

''I'm trying to exercise self control.''

The entendre made her smile as she lifted the candy to his mouth. ''Surely it's okay to give in to temptation every once in a while.''

He let her pop the candy into his mouth. Her fingertips lingered against his lips for a moment, brushing across them like a fleeting kiss. He almost choked on the fudge. He was forced to wash it down with a gulp of coffee.

''Am I making you nervous again?'' she asked in a murmur.

''No.'' Finally surrendering to the instincts he'd been fighting, he set his coffee mug beside hers and then turned to reach for her. ''But maybe *you* should be nervous.''

''You don't scare me, Dan Meadows,'' she said, wrapping her arms around his neck.

Even though he knew he should, he didn't try to argue with her any further. She wouldn't have listened to him, anyway.

The kiss flavored with chocolate and coffee, lasted a very long time. When it finally ended, their relationship had changed irrevocably.

Maybe Lindsey should have spent more time getting to know Dr. McAdoo. Probably that would have been the wisest, most logical decision for her to make.

But she'd chosen to come to Dan instead. And for once he wasn't going to try to change her mind.

He wasn't a saint. And this time Lindsey had pushed his willpower beyond its limits.

A surge of strength carried him to his feet, Lindsey held high against his chest. She gave a laughing gasp and clung to him, her gaze locked trustingly with his.

"Sure you don't want to change your mind?" he asked her, his voice a strained growl.

She only smiled and tightened her arms around his neck. "I've been waiting much too long for this to change my mind now."

He pressed his mouth to hers again, then moved toward the bedroom. He wondered if she could feel his heart pounding against his chest. Doubts still hovered somewhere in the back of his mind, but they'd been pushed aside by reckless anticipation. He'd given her more than enough chances to back out. Now he was calling her bluff.

The bedroom was small, dimly lit, as sparsely decorated as the rest of the place. Hardly the most romantic setting for this momentous step, but it would have to do. Besides, Dan thought as he lowered Lindsey to the clean, inexpensive white sheets, she might as well find out exactly what she was getting into with him.

This was who he was, take him or leave him. And he found himself fervently hoping that Lindsey would decide to take him. All of him.

Lindsey found it rather flattering that Dan's hands shook as he fumbled with her clothes. She never would have imagined that she could make him tremble.

She grew self-conscious when he unsnapped her black lace bra to reveal the slight curves beneath. ''Small,'' she murmured with a wry smile.

He covered her breasts with his hands, his palms warm and deliciously rough against her tender skin. ''Perfect,'' he assured her, and she heard only sincerity in his deep voice.

He lowered his head to take her right nipple gently between his teeth. She felt all the air leave her lungs. There wasn't enough breath left for her to even gasp his name. He used his lips and tongue to trace her body, his teeth to thrill her. There was no longer any awkwardness in his movements—and now she was the one who trembled.

Growing impatient, she tugged at his shirt. It wasn't fair that she was stripped to tiny panties while he was still fully covered. She wanted the same freedom to touch and explore that he enjoyed.

The body she revealed was lean and sinewy. His tan attested to the hours he'd spent outside, and scattered scars served as evidence of the adventures that had filled those hours. Dan had been a bit of a daredevil in his youth; he and B.J. had rarely met a challenge they hadn't tried to conquer. She'd been so in awe of Dan then.

She hadn't changed much in that respect, she admitted ruefully, holding her breath as she ran her hands down his muscular back to the waistband of his jeans.

Dan returned his attention to her mouth, kissing her slowly. Thoroughly. Intimately.

He kissed her like a lover.

Finally releasing her mouth so they could breathe, he lifted his head. ''You're still sure about this?''

Why was he having such a difficult time believing that she knew exactly what she was doing? How could she possibly regret something she'd been dreaming about for so long?

She cupped his face in her hands and looked him straight in the eyes. ''I am absolutely, positively, unequivocally sure.''

''That sounds pretty certain,'' he murmured with a faint smile.

''I'm glad you're finally getting that straight. Now would you please go back to what you were doing?''

''I'll try to remember where I left off.''

Putting her mouth to his, she spoke against his lips. ''See if this jogs your memory.''

She kissed him without holding anything back. She kissed him until he didn't have enough breath left to ask any more foolish questions. Which was just as well: by the time that explosive embrace ended, she couldn't have formed a coherent answer had her life depended on it.

Being the careful, thoughtful, well-prepared type that he was, Dan had protection stashed in his nightstand. Lindsey waited impatiently for him to return to her, and greeted him eagerly when he did. Dan took another long, leisurely tour of her body, dropping kisses from the tip of her nose to the tops of her toes, missing very few spots in between. He found erotic places she hadn't even known were there, and then aptly demonstrated just how wonderful those places could feel.

As much as he would let her, Lindsey returned the favor—kissing, stroking and nibbling any part of him she could reach. She was rewarded with an occasional appreciative rumble from deep in his chest.

The ultimate reward came when Dan's patience ran out and his movements grew more intense, more focused on a final goal. He came to her with a murmur of welcome. There was no shock of strangeness when he surged into her, but a rush of joy, an almost overwhelming sense of rightness and familiarity. Of finally coming home.

So long, Lindsey thought, arching to take him deeper. She had been waiting for so long....

Even as waves of pleasure washed over her, temporarily shutting down all her other senses, she was aware of her delight that Dan had finally realized they belonged together.

He gasped her name when he climaxed only moments later. It wasn't exactly a declaration of his feelings for her, but she would settle for what she could get. At least for now.

Dan wasn't sure exactly what he was feeling as he lay on his back in his bed, staring at the shadowy ceiling above him. So many emotions waged inside him that it was difficult to isolate and identify them. He knew that fear lurked somewhere among them.

Lindsey lay with her head nestled into his shoulder. Though she was being very still, he didn't think she was asleep.

He didn't have a clue what she thinking.

She was so light against him, her figure slender and willowy. He knew now that there was a lot of passion packed into that small package. She held a lot of power in her small hands—the capability to bring him to his knees if he wasn't careful.

''You're getting nervous again,'' she murmured, making him wonder if mind reading was among her powers.

''I'm not nervous,'' he lied—just in case his thoughts were still a mystery to him.

She laughed softly. ''Liar.''

She was only guessing, he assured himself, letting the accusation pass unanswered.

Lindsey shifted into a more comfortable position against him. Her soft bare skin brushing against his caused an immediate, and somewhat startling, reaction in his groin.

He cleared his throat. ''Are you, uh, hungry or anything?''

''No, not really.'' The very primness of her response let him know she was still amused by him.

''I'm glad you're finding all this so entertaining,'' he muttered.

She reached up to stroke his evening-rough skin. ''When I'm happy, I can't help laughing.''

His momentary irritation vanished. Lindsey's happiness was, after all, extremely important to him. If laughing at him made her happy, then he might as well take it gracefully.

She brushed her lips against his throat, lingering to plant a kiss just beneath his ear. This time he made no effort to hide his response. One smooth move, and he had her on top of him. She gave another startled, breathless laugh, then covered his mouth with hers.

* * *

Lindsey was awakened by the shrill ring of a telephone. Her first instinct was to grope toward her nightstand. When her hand encountered empty air where her phone should be, she opened her eyes, only then realizing that she wasn't in her own bed.

At the same time that fact occurred to her, she heard Dan's deep voice saying, "Hello?"

Moments later he sat up in the bed, the sheets falling to his waist. Holding the bedclothes to her chin, Lindsey pushed herself onto one elbow, peering blearily at the clock. It was only 5:00 a.m. Poor Dan—how often did he get roused out of bed like this? His was definitely not a forty-hour-a-week job. She didn't fault him for that; she admired him for taking his responsibilities so seriously.

He hung up and turned to her. His voice was still gruff from sleep when he said, "I've got to go."

"Not another fire?"

He swung his legs over the side of the bed, reaching for his clothes. "No."

Something in his tone told her she would very likely be interested on a professional level in the call he'd just received. And Dan knew it. "What's going on?"

He answered with obvious reluctance. "Eddie Stamps has turned up. He's holed up in his bedroom with a gun."

"Oh, no." She jumped from the bed and started groping for her clothes. "I guess it will look better if we take separate cars. I'll meet you there."

"There's no need for you to go there at all," he said, shoving his feet into his boots. "The kid has a gun, Lindsey."

"And I intend to stay out of range. But I will be there, Dan. This is my job."

"It's my job, not yours. It's too dangerous for you to be there. I'll let you know what happens."

"My job is to be on the scene covering the news in person whenever possible."

"Yeah, well, you're still wearing the bandage from the last time you did that, or have you forgotten?"

"I haven't forgotten, and I promise I'll be more careful this time. But I am going. You can't stop me."

"Damn it."

The curse was basically an acknowledgment that she was right about him not being able to keep her away. He could order her to a safe distance once she arrived at the scene; he could even keep her off Mrs. Stamps's property, but he couldn't stop her from hovering in the background. And she suspected he knew very well that she would even risk disobeying his direct orders if she thought they interfered with her freedom to report the news.

"Just stay out of my way," he warned.

She gave him a cheeky smile. "Yes, Chief."

His only response was a growl.

For the sake of discretion, Lindsey gave Dan a ten-minute head start. She used that time to retrieve her camera from the trunk of her car and make sure it had film and batteries. The Edstown *Evening Star* had a limited staff; she didn't have a photographer to summon. She could call Riley, of course, but there was no need to rouse him just yet. She could handle this assignment herself.

During the drive to Opal Stamps's house, she used her cell phone to call her boss and editor. Cameron answered on the second ring, sounding wide awake. She identified herself and rapidly informed him where she was going. It turned out he already knew about the situation.

"Opal Stamps just called Serena," he explained. "She wants to retain her as a lawyer for Eddie. Opal told us Eddie's locked in his room, and she thought he'd be more cooperative if he has a legal representative on his side. Serena's getting dressed, and then she and I are heading over there. No way I'm letting her go into that situation alone, though she has informed me she's perfectly capable of doing so. I tried calling you to send you to the scene, but I got your machine when I called your house and no answer on your cell phone. I was just about to call Riley."

"No need. I'm almost there." She saw no reason to explain why she hadn't been home to answer her phone, or that her cell phone had been left overnight in her car.

"All right. But use your head, will you? If bullets start flying, I don't want to hear you jumped in front of one just to get a better angle on the story."

"Very funny, boss."

"I'm not trying to be funny. I'm telling you to be careful."

"Okay, I'll be careful. See you in a little while." She disconnected the call as she parked her car on the side of the road beside Opal Stamps's house, directly behind a dark sedan she recognized as Dr. Frank Purtle's. A marked patrol car, its lights flashing, sat in the driveway, and Dan's truck was parked next to it.

Climbing out of her car, Lindsey slipped the neck

strap to her camera over her head, slid her notebook into the pocket of the jacket she'd retrieved from her back seat and moved to join a group of three men standing in the driveway behind the patrol car. A security light on a pole above them gave just enough light for her to identify everyone in one swift glance—Officers Billy Braden and Joe Elrod, and Dr. Frank Purtle. She didn't see Dan. ''What are you doing here?'' she asked the physician everyone knew as ''Dr. Frank.''

He nodded toward the house. ''Mrs. Stamps called me. She wanted me to sedate the boy, but he won't let me near him. I decided to stay awhile—just in case I'm needed.''

She devoutly hoped he wouldn't be needed to treat any gunshot wounds. Turning to Billy Braden, she asked, ''Where's Dan?''

The officer—a distant cousin of Dan's—replied, his broad face somber. He's inside with Mrs. Stamps. They're trying to talk the boy out of his room, but he's not having any of it. He keeps telling them to stay away from him or he'll shoot himself.''

Lindsey grimaced. ''He's feeling hopeless. Cornered.''

''Cornered animals can be very dangerous,'' Dr. Frank observed.

''Eddie isn't an animal. He's just a scared and mixed-up kid.''

''That *kid* could be an arsonist,'' Officer Joe Elrod—the mayor's nephew—growled. ''And if he set the fire that killed Truman Kellogg, he's a murderer, as well.''

''Careful what you're saying, Joe.'' Her hands in

the pockets of her leather coat, Serena North spoke as she approached, her husband at her heels. "At this point, as far as I know, there's no evidence that Eddie has committed any crime. And we still don't know that Kellogg's death was related to any of the other fires."

Joe scowled. "You representing him, Serena?"

"I don't know yet. But I do know that there is a presumption of innocence at this point. Remember?"

Lindsey piped in. "I can't believe Eddie would deliberately kill anyone. Even if he *did* set that fire—which, as Serena pointed out, we can't prove yet—he must not have known Mr. Kellogg was there."

Her attention drawn to the house again, she took a step in that direction. "Maybe there's something I could do to help. Eddie knows me, and he always seems to like me. Maybe I could talk to him...."

She didn't like the thought of Dan being in there with a terrified young man with a gun. If anything went wrong...

"I don't think so." Billy caught her arm. "Dan told me to keep you out here."

Lindsey scowled, her concern for Dan making her temper flare in response to being kept away from him. "You really want to move that hand, Billy, before Dr. Frank has to sew it back on for you."

Because she'd once blackened his eye—she'd been five and he seven at the time, and he'd thought it would be fun to kick over a block tower she'd very carefully constructed—the officer released her rather hastily. He kept his voice stern. "You know better than to threaten an officer of the law."

"All I want to do is find out what—" She stopped

when she suddenly spotted Eddie Stamps looking back at her from his bedroom window. Tentatively, she gave him a smile and a wave of her hand.

The curtain was abruptly closed again.

"Just let me go knock on the door," she said to Billy, haunted by the desperate expression on the boy's face. "If Dan won't let me in, I'll stay out of the way."

"I'm sorry, Lindsey, but Dan directly instructed me to keep you away from the house. You know how mad he can get if his orders aren't obeyed."

She gritted her teeth. "You know how mad *I* can get when someone interferes with me getting my story."

He seemed to pale a little, but he held his ground. "Given a choice of having you mad at me or Dan, I'll take you."

Secretly she understood, of course. Dan's temper—quiet and icy in contrast to her own somewhat more volatile outbursts—was something to be avoided whenever possible all right. But she needed very badly to know he was all right. To help keep him safe, if possible—even though she knew he wouldn't appreciate her worrying about him this way. "I'll tell him I didn't give you a choice. Just let me—"

The front door to the house opened and Opal Stamps stepped out onto the porch. Wearing a shabby flannel bathrobe, she wrung her hands, looking drawn and anxious. "Lindsey? You out here?"

Dan followed Opal out, placing a hand on her shoulder. "Mrs. Stamps—"

The woman shrugged him away as Lindsey stepped

forward. "My boy wants to talk to you," Opal said to Lindsey.

Lindsey took another step toward the house. "He wants to talk to *me?*"

"Lindsey, this is not a good idea," Dan said. "Eddie's distraught. Irrational. I've called for a professional negotiator. A psychiatrist. He'll be here in another half hour or so."

"Eddie ain't going to be alive in a half hour!" Opal whirled to face Dan. "He said if we don't let him talk to Lindsey, he'll pull that trigger. He's upset enough to do it."

Stepping onto the porch, Lindsey placed a hand on the woman's arm. "I'll talk to him, Mrs. Stamps. But I'm not sure what I can do to help."

"Nothing." Dan shook his head stubbornly. "There's not a thing you can do. The kid's got a gun, and he's on the verge of a breakdown. His mother and I have both tried to talk to him, but he isn't listening to reason. If you slip up and say the wrong thing, he's liable to go over the edge. I'm not willing to risk that."

"He just wants to talk to you, Lindsey." Opal's tone and her expression were pleading. "He always liked you. He'll listen to you."

"I'm coming in." Lindsey moved forward, pausing only when Cameron touched her arm.

"Be careful," he said.

She nodded. "I will."

Dan's scowl was fierce. "Damn it, Lindsey, will you listen to reason?"

"We don't have a choice, Dan," she answered, gazing up at him as she approached the doorway he was blocking with his body. "I couldn't live with myself if Eddie kills himself because I turned down his request to talk. Could you?"

He sighed, and his expression told her that he knew it would be futile to argue with her any longer. "I'm going in with you."

"If he'll let you, that's fine with me."

Serena and Cameron followed them to the porch. "Tell him I'm here, Lindsey," Serena urged. "Tell him I'm on his side, and I'll help him, whatever he's done."

Lindsey nodded. "I'll tell him."

Drawing a deep breath, she moved closer to Dan, her eyes locked with his. Very reluctantly he moved aside to let her enter the house.

Chapter Twelve

The last time Dan had been this scared, a brick wall had just exploded all over Lindsey. He felt much the same way now as he stared at the closed door that separated him from Lindsey and a desperate teenager with a loaded .45.

Dan had done everything short of arresting her to keep her from going into that room, but she hadn't listened to warnings or threats. When Eddie had tearfully begged her through the door to come in and listen to what he had to say, there was nothing short of physical violence that could have stopped her—and Dan had even threatened that.

"He won't hurt her," Opal assured him as he restlessly prowled the dingy living room. "My boy's not dangerous. He's just scared because some people are starting to say he had something to do with those fires."

Dan wasn't quite sure how that rumor had gotten out; he suspected some of Eddie's classmates had started it—possibly someone who had reason to believe it was true. ''I told Eddie I would listen to him—that I'd give him a chance to tell his side. Why wouldn't he talk to me?''

Twisting her hands in front of her, Opal eyed him nervously. ''Well, you can be sort of…''

Dan whirled toward her impatiently. *''What?''*

She took a step backward. ''Intimidating.''

''That's ridiculous,'' he snapped, stamping to the other side of the room.

Even as he considered and rejected several possibilities for storming Eddie's bedroom and rescuing Lindsey, he caught a glimpse of his reflection in a cheaply framed mirror hanging on a wall. The dark scowl he'd already been wearing deepened. Hell. He *did* look intimidating. Picturing Lindsey's pretty, smiling face next to his own, he could definitely understand why Eddie had chosen to confide in her.

Which didn't mean Dan had to like it. Or approve.

He couldn't believe he'd let her go in there alone. What had he been thinking? How could he have allowed his professional judgment to be swayed by the look in her eyes, the tone of her voice? When it came to Lindsey, he lost all objectivity in his work—and that wasn't good.

He glanced at his watch, noting that the second hand seemed to be hardly moving. He was giving her one more minute, he decided, and then he was going to figure out a way to get in there.

Forty-five seconds had passed when the bedroom door suddenly opened.

Lindsey stepped out first, carrying the .45 in her right hand as gingerly as if it might explode without warning. His homely face red and streaked with tears, Eddie shuffled out after her, hanging his head like a six-foot-tall kindergartener.

"He wants to talk," Lindsey announced. "I think Serena should be present."

Opal rushed toward the door. "I'll get her."

Dan took a step toward Lindsey and held out his hand—which, he noted, was not entirely steady. She placed the gun in his palm, looking greatly relieved to be rid of it.

He wanted to hold her, just to reassure himself that she was safe and unharmed. Instead, he stuck the gun in the back of his waistband and forced himself to turn away from her. "Let's take a ride to the station where we can talk, Eddie," he said, trying to keep his voice measured and even. As unintimidating as possible.

"I'd like to talk to him before anyone questions him," Serena said from the doorway, giving Eddie an encouraging smile. "I'll follow the patrol car to the police station, and we'll talk there," she assured him. "Your mother can join us, if you want, or we'll talk in private. Whichever makes you more comfortable."

Eddie nodded, cast a wary glance toward Dan, then sidled toward Serena.

Dan's two officers moved into the doorway, stepping toward Eddie. Joe was reaching for the handcuffs on his belt.

"Oh, it really isn't necessary to cuff him, is it, Dan?" Lindsey asked quickly.

Dan leveled a look at Eddie. "You going to give my officers any trouble?"

"N-no, sir," he stammered.

"Then we'll skip the cuffs. Go on, now. Do what the officers tell you."

Nodding dejectedly, the young man allowed himself to be escorted out, Serena and Cameron following closely behind.

"I don't know why you've got to arrest him," Opal complained to Dan. "He didn't hurt no one."

"He had a gun, Mrs. Stamps."

"But he wasn't threatening to hurt anyone but himself."

"We're just taking him in for questioning at this point. Whatever he's done—or hasn't done—it's obvious that your son needs help."

She couldn't argue with that. "I'll get dressed," she muttered, moving toward the hallway with dispirited steps.

"I'll drive her to the station when she's ready, Dan," Dr. Frank volunteered.

Dan nodded, moving toward the doorway. "I suppose you're going to the station, too?" he asked Lindsey as she fell into step at his side.

"Of course."

"Good. I want to know everything the kid said to you."

She lifted her eyebrows as they moved onto the porch. "Some of what he said was in confidence."

"You're not his attorney. Confidence rules don't apply here."

"A reporter does not have to divulge information

given off the record,'' she replied, familiar obstinacy in the set of her chin.

''I'm not asking just any reporter, damn it,'' he snapped, stopping beside the driver's door of his truck. ''I'm asking *you* to tell me what he said.''

That stubborn chin of hers rose even higher. ''My personal relationship with you will get you some things, Chief, but it won't get you inside information concerning my work.''

He recognized the pointed paraphrasing of the words he'd said to her that Saturday in her kitchen, when he'd fixed her leaky faucet but refused to share information about the arson investigation. He had to keep a firm hold on his temper.

''I'll see you at the station,'' he said, jerking open the driver's door of his truck. ''And if Eddie said anything to you that is relevant to my investigation, you'll tell me even if I have to get a judge to order you to cooperate!''

''Reporters go to jail before they betray their sources,'' she reminded him, her own temper evident from the flush on her cheeks.

''Don't tempt me.'' He climbed into the truck and slammed the door.

He didn't know if he was ready for the roller-coaster ride that a relationship with Lindsey would keep him on. Just in the past few hours, his emotions toward her had ranged from passion to terror to exasperation.

Maybe his personal life had become routine and predictable during the past couple of years, but at least it had been relatively peaceful and comfortable. He had no doubt that Lindsey would change all that, turning his comfortable routines upside down. She already had, for that matter.

He simply didn't know if he was ready for this—or if Lindsey would be content for long with a man who preferred his personal life to be as unexciting as possible in contrast to his demanding career.

Fortunately it wasn't necessary for Dan to have to subpoena Lindsey for information. Eddie repeated every word he'd told Lindsey—first to Serena and then to Dan. He admitted setting the fires around Edstown, but he fervently denied having anything to do with the one in which Truman Kellogg had died. Nor, he insisted, had he been responsible for the fire that had destroyed the insurance company earlier that week.

''Do you believe him?'' Lindsey asked Dan over coffee in his trailer later that day. It was just past noon—several hours after Eddie had been taken to the police station where he was still being held pending a bail hearing the next day. She and Dan had both been busy during those hours, only now having a chance to relax and have something to eat.

''I don't know.'' Dan gazed into the coffee mug cradled between his hands as if he could find an answer there. ''We know he set most of the fires. It's a bit suspicious that the ones he denies are the ones with the most serious consequences. All he's claiming are the old, long-vacant buildings.''

She remembered the desperation with which Eddie had repeatedly assured her that he would not have risked having anyone hurt by the fires he'd set. ''I know it sounds hard to believe—but he seemed so sincere, Dan. He gave so many details about the fires he did claim, but he knew nothing about the others."

"Not that he admitted, anyway. While there's still some doubt about the cause of the fire at Kellogg's fishing cabin, we know the insurance company was deliberately torched. Don't you find it hard to believe we've got two arsonists operating in Edstown?"

"Well, sure," she admitted. "But it *could* be a copycat, couldn't it? One of Eddie's friends, maybe, who wanted to prove he was just as dangerous. Maybe?"

Dan shrugged. "I guess it's a possibility."

He didn't sound convinced. Lindsey wasn't sure she was, either. She wanted to believe Eddie's fire-setting spree had been a symbolic cry for emotional help, that he'd been careful no one was harmed by what might have seemed to him like victimless crimes. But she was as skeptical as Dan that there were suddenly two serial arsonists in a town that had never even seen one before this.

Dan refilled his coffee mug, then returned to his seat. His thoughts were obviously still on his work, giving her a chance to study him across the table.

Because they'd been roused out of bed so early and so abruptly, neither of them had had a chance to shower. Dan's jaw was covered with a two-day growth of beard that she found very attractive—but then she found almost everything about Dan appealing. He'd run his hands through his dark-brown hair so much that it was wildly tousled—reminding her of the way it had looked after she'd run *her* hands through it. He wore a denim shirt with the sleeves rolled up the forearms, a pair of jeans and his battered boots. A casual and infinitely masculine look that was incredibly sexy in her admittedly biased opinion.

She gave a fleeting thought to her own appearance. She hadn't had a chance to do more than run a brush through her hair, leaving it in the somewhat spiky style she'd favored before her makeover. There'd been no time for makeup, and she wore the same striped sweater and jeans she'd had on yesterday. Sometime during the morning she'd removed the bandage from her forehead. It had become annoying to her, and the shallow wound beneath it had healed enough that she didn't think the bandage was necessary any longer. So here she sat, rumpled, bruised and unadorned—hardly at her best.

No wonder Dan's attention was wholly focused on work at the moment.

Remembering the flash of tempers between them as they'd left Opal Stamps's house earlier, she wondered if he was still annoyed by the exchange. She hadn't given it much thought until now, since they'd always clashed quite vocally when it came to their jobs. She didn't expect that to change just because she and Dan had become lovers. Surely he didn't expect her to perform her work any less conscientiously just to please him.

''Dan?''

''Mmm?''

''Have I told you yet that last night was spectacular?''

That brought his attention abruptly back to her. He blinked a couple of times, seeming to grope for an appropriate answer. And then he just gave up and sighed. ''You really enjoy catching me off guard like that, don't you?''

She dimpled at him. ''Yes.''

His expression softened a little, and he returned the smile with a slight one of his own. ''Was I ignoring you?''

''Let's just say I think we both need a little break from work.''

''You're probably right. You need some rest. You, um, didn't get much sleep last night.''

''Neither did you,'' she reminded him, studying the dark circles beneath his eyes.

''I'm not the one who was taken to a hospital emergency room just two days ago.''

''Don't start fussing about that again. You know I've completely recovered from that incident.''

The look he gave her made her aware of every bruise she still bore from that ''incident.'' ''Not quite completely.''

''I suppose I could use a little nap. Care to join me?''

He cleared his throat. ''I, uh, have some things I really should be doing.''

It looked as though it was up to her to take the lead again, she thought with a wry shake of her head. Honestly, Dan was so skittish about their relationship that she couldn't help mentally comparing him to an animal that had been abused. Convincing him to fully trust her was going to take both love and patience. Fortunately, when it came to Dan, she seemed to have a big supply of both.

She stood and slowly rounded the table, her gaze locked with his. ''It's Sunday afternoon. The arsonist you've been chasing is behind bars, your weekend officers are on duty, and most offices are closed until tomorrow morning. There's nothing you need to do that can't wait a few more hours—is there?''

To her very great satisfaction, he pushed his coffee mug aside, rose and jerked her into his arms. ''No,'' he muttered, his lips an inch away from hers. ''There's nothing that can't wait. Except for this.''

He crushed her mouth beneath his. Lindsey stretched up to meet him more fully, locking her arms around his neck, pressing her soft body eagerly closer to his harder one.

As Dan swung her into his arms and headed for the bedroom, she held on in heady anticipation. She had no doubt that Dan was thinking now about nothing but her.

Lindsey was sitting on Dan's couch, reading the Sunday edition of the state-wide newspaper, when someone knocked on the front door. She lowered the paper and frowned over it. Through the thin mobile home walls, she could hear the shower running behind her; Dan had just stepped into it. Her hair was still wet from her own shower. She'd donned her shirt, jeans and socks, but was wearing no makeup or shoes.

She was well aware of the impression someone could get from seeing her this way in his house.

She was tempted to ignore the knock and pretend no one was home. But Dan's truck was sitting in the driveway, as was her car. It was obvious someone was here. Besides which, when someone knocked on

Dan's door, there was always a chance it could be a police emergency.

Hoping she'd be able to bluff her way through whatever resulted from her decision, she set the paper aside and rose to answer the door.

She knew when she identified the caller that bluffing was not going to be an option.

Riley took a moment to give her a slow once-over before speaking. "Hey, Linds."

She curled her toes self-consciously in her socks. "Hey, Riley."

"Dan home?"

"He's, uh, in the shower."

"I see." Riley stuck his tongue in his cheek and glanced at her damp hair. "Am I interrupting something?"

"Of course not. I was just reading the newspaper. Come in."

He stepped inside, closing the door behind him.

"You want some coffee? I just made a fresh pot."

"No, thanks. Actually, I just stopped by to get an update on the arson investigation. My uncle is anxious to find out if Eddie Stamps has confessed to setting the fire that killed Truman Kellogg."

Riley's uncle, Bud O'Neal, had been one of Truman's best friends. Another old friend, Stan Holt, had owned the insurance company that had been destroyed in the last fire. Nearly everyone in town had been affected in some way by the string of arsons, Lindsey thought sadly. Could Eddie really have been responsible for all that destruction?

She settled on the couch again while Riley sank into a chair nearby. "Eddie unequivocably denied having anything to do with the fire that killed Truman—or the one that destroyed the insurance company. Of course, as Dan pointed out, the two fires he disavowed are the ones with the most serious consequences."

"I see. So...are you waiting to interview Dan after his shower?"

She gave him a chiding look. "I think you know very well I'm not here on business."

"I was trying to give you a graceful out."

"You mean you don't have any acerbic comments to make?"

"No. Not about this."

She was a bit surprised by the seriousness of his tone. "What do you mean?"

Notoriously wary about getting involved in other people's personal affairs, Riley answered a bit reluctantly. "You know I'm very fond of both you and Dan. I've always admired the way you've been able to stay good friends despite your professional differences. I'd hate to see anything happen to change that."

Typically candid with her friends, Lindsey said, "Look, Riley, you have to know I've been crazy about Dan for years. I just finally decided it was time to do something about it."

"*You* decided? How does Dan feel about this?"

"You know Dan. He's being very...cautious."

"I'm glad to hear somebody is."

Tilting her head, she studied him in bemusement. "It isn't like you to be so pessimistic."

The look he gave her in return was apologetic. "I

suppose it could work out. But surely even you can see there are a lot of strikes against this relationship.''

''Such as?''

''He's a lot older than you.''

''Ten years. It isn't as if he's twice my age.''

''He was burned very badly by the fiasco with Melanie. He's still carrying a lot of baggage from that.''

''I know. I can deal with it.''

''And what about you? How do you know that what you're feeling for Dan isn't just left-over adolescent infatuation? Last I heard, you had big plans to move to a larger city to pursue your journalism career more ambitiously. You and I both know you're too good to be writing local-interest stories for the *Evening Star*. How long do you think it will be before you start getting restless again? I think *itchy* was the word you used at the party the other night.''

Suddenly aware that the shower had stopped running, and uncertain how long it had been off, Lindsey spoke a bit more softly. ''I know what I feel for Dan, and it isn't infatuation. I don't think a high-profile reporting career is such a big sacrifice in comparison.''

Apparently Riley had offered all the advice and warnings he intended to give. He merely shrugged and said, ''You know where to find me if you need me.''

While she wasn't pleased with the lack of confidence in his tone, she was still touched by the sincerity of his offer. ''I know. Thanks, Riley.''

''Yeah, well...good luck.''

It was obvious that he thought she was going to need all the luck she could get.

He stood. "You know, I think I'll clear out now. I really just wanted an update on the arson case, but I can get that later."

"There's really no need for you to rush off. Dan should be out any minute."

"Tell him I'll call him later, okay?"

She followed him to the door. "Riley—"

He brushed her jaw with his knuckles. "See you later, Linds. And, needless to say, I won't mention this to anyone."

"I appreciate it."

She closed the door behind him and sighed. And then she turned and gasped when she saw Dan standing in the doorway. "Oh. I—"

His expression gave nothing away. "Was that Riley?"

"Yes. He wanted an update on the arson case. He said he'll call you later."

"Okay. Do I smell coffee?"

"Yes, I just made some." Had he overheard any of her conversation with Riley? She couldn't read a thing in his expression.

"Let's have a sandwich or something, and then I'd like to run by the station again. There are a few things I need to do there."

She nodded and followed him into the kitchen, telling herself she must be just imagining that a new barrier had just gone up between herself and Dan.

Chapter Thirteen

"Dan, you have a call on line two. It's B. J. Gray."

Dan frowned at the intercom on his desk before he responded, "Thanks, Hazel."

It was with some reluctance that he picked up the receiver. Two weeks had passed since he and Lindsey had become lovers, and this was the first time he'd spoken to her brother since. He couldn't help but feel awkward. "Hi, B.J. How's it going?"

"I'm doing well. How about you? Any new developments in the arson case?"

"Yeah. We caught our firebug last week."

"No kidding. Anyone I know?"

"It's Merle and Opal Stamps's son, Eddie. He's eighteen. A senior in high school."

"A high school kid caused all that damage?" B.J. sounded stunned.

"And managed to elude us for almost six months," Dan agreed grimly.

"Have you got a confession?"

"He's going for a plea bargain. He's confessing to all but two of the fires. Says he had nothing to do with the one at Truman Kellogg's fishing cabin. Since we have no evidence that he was involved in that one—not even proof that it actually was arson—there's really no way we can pin it on Eddie. At this the cause of that fire is listed as undetermined."

"You mean the Stamps kid might get away with murder?"

"Negligent homicide, possibly. But there's nothing I can do about it, B.J. I made the arrest. Now it's up to the courts. He should get a fairly tough punishment for the fires he's admitting to—along with some intensive counseling, I hope—but he won't do time for Kellogg's death unless more evidence turns up. And frankly I'm not expecting that to happen."

"Well, at least the kid won't be setting any more fires. That's got to be a load off your shoulders."

"It's a relief to everyone. We've all been getting tense, wondering when he was going to strike again, hoping no one else would be hurt."

"So, have you seen my sister lately? I've been trying to reach her for a couple of weeks, but we keep missing each other. Except for a few short e-mails, I've barely heard from her since I was home last."

Dan glanced at yesterday's newspaper, which was spread out on his desk. The front page bore an article with Lindsey's byline—an excellent, in-depth interview with students and teachers who knew Eddie Stamps from school. Below that was another story she'd written—full coverage of an Edstown High School beauty pageant.

Inside the *Evening Star* were articles about local kids who'd been named "citizens of the month" at the elementary and middle schools, an interview with the mayor about a community effort to get a new traffic light on Elm Street, coverage of the grand opening of a new video store, and a whimsical little piece about the old gentleman who'd been a crossing guard in front of the elementary school for more than twenty years. Lindsey had written most of those articles, leaving coverage of local ball games, fishing tournaments and city council meetings for Riley, and recipes and household hints for Ella Painter, a retired home economics teacher.

"Lindsey's been pretty busy lately," he said to B.J. "Always chasing stories for the paper."

B.J. chuckled. "I still have the paper mailed to me, just to keep abreast of Edstown gossip. Lindsey pretty much writes the whole thing, doesn't she?"

"Pretty much."

"I will say that the quality of the paper has gone up considerably since Cameron North took over as managing editor. He gives the staff a lot more freedom to cover the news than Marvin did."

"Yeah. Marvin was always afraid of making waves or ticking off someone influential. Cameron says he's putting out a newspaper, not a piece of PR fluff."

"I know Lindsey's much happier working for him than she was Marvin. Still, has she said any more to you about getting a job in a bigger city?"

"Not lately." Dan folded the paper and set it aside. "I've told her several times that her talents are underutilized here. She could work anywhere she wants.''

''Yeah, I've told her the same thing. Of course, being the overprotective big brother that I am, I rather like having her there in Edstown where I know she's safe and sheltered from the big, bad world. And she has you there to watch out for her in my place.''

Dan grimaced. ''I'm not a baby-sitter, B.J. And Lindsey doesn't need one.''

''I know.'' His friend sounded rueful. ''She tells me often enough that I've got to stop treating her like a kid. She's closer to thirty than twenty now, she's always reminding me. But, you know how it is. I still think of her as my little sister.''

Dan swallowed.

''Oh, hell,'' B.J. said after a moment. ''I just want her to be happy. If that means she should move to a bigger city, then I'll give her my full encouragement.''

''I'm sure she appreciates your support.''

''So, you've seen her lately?''

''Oh, sure. I see her often.''

''And she looks well to you? She's really doing okay since Dad died?''

''She's fine. Looks great. And she seems happy.''

''Good. You would tell me if there was any reason to be concerned.''

Dan rubbed his forehead, which was beginning to ache dully. ''Yeah. Of course I would.''

''Is she dating anyone? Surely she isn't working *all* the time.''

Dan had probably been more uncomfortably self-conscious at some point in the past couple of years—

but not that he could remember. ‘‘I doubt that she would appreciate us gossiping about her behind her back.’’

B.J. laughed. ‘‘You’re probably right. I imagine she’d tear a strip or two off my hide if she thought I was checking up on her. And she’d be especially mad about me asking *you* about her social life, considering the giant crush she once had on you.’’

This was the third person in the past month to refer to Lindsey’s girlhood infatuation. First Marjorie, then Riley—in a conversation Dan had accidentally overheard—and now B.J.

‘‘Since both of us have reason to be wary of Lindsey’s temper, we’d better change the subject,’’ he said, attempting to inject a note of humor in his voice. ‘‘How are things in—where the hell are you these days?’’

‘‘I’m in Seoul at the moment. I’ll probably be here another six weeks or so, and then maybe I can get home for a visit.’’

Six weeks. As B.J. chattered on about his recent activities, Dan wondered what would be going on between him and Lindsey in six weeks. Would their affair be over by then or still hovering in this tentative limbo? It might be that B.J. would never even know about it—which would suit Dan just fine if things didn’t work out. It would be bad enough to lose Lindsey. Ruining his longtime friendship with B.J. would be almost, if not quite, as devastating.

Dan was driving Lindsey crazy. Not a new development—he’d been doing so for years—but this was different. He should certainly know how she felt about him by now, but his feelings about her were more of a mystery than ever.

At his suggestion they were extremely discreet about the new direction their relationship had taken. In public they acted no differently toward each other than they ever had. She doubted that anyone—with the exception of Riley, of course—could tell that she and Dan had become lovers.

He said they deserved privacy during these early stages of their romance. They were both aware that if word got out about them, everyone they knew would be watching them, speculating and making comments. Lindsey could see Dan's point—and yet sometimes she wanted very badly to shout from the rooftops that she was in love and deliriously happy. She'd have been perfectly content to run a front-page story about it with a banner headline—but if Dan wanted discretion, she could be patient. For now.

She knew he was still smarting from his very public breakup with Melanie. She certainly didn't want to remind him of that unhappy time.

Because of his near obsession with their privacy, they saw each other rarely during the three weeks that followed that first night. Both were busy with work, of course—a perfectly legitimate excuse—but Dan was also concerned about being seen too often at Lindsey's house or vice versa. He knew too well how closely the neighbors monitored their activities, and how quickly gossip spread from the beauty parlor throughout the rest of the town.

When he did deem it safe for them to be together, he usually came to her house. Sometimes they would talk for a while, usually about work or local events, but it wouldn't be long before they would fall into each other's arms. The passion between them had not diminished since that first night. It seemed, instead, to grow stronger each time they were together.

Every time they made love, Lindsey grew more optimistic about their future. Despite Dan's reticence about expressing his emotions, she couldn't believe he could make love with her with such intensity unless he felt the same way she did. Could he?

If only she could be patient until he was ready for the next step. She certainly wouldn't want to scare him off at this point. And yet...she'd had to make the first move last time. She supposed it was possible that she would have to do so again.

If only she could wait until the time was right.

Late in April Dan had to attend a four-day conference in Dallas. Lindsey missed him terribly while he was gone. She'd hoped he would call, but he didn't. She chided herself for spending those evenings waiting hopefully by the telephone—but she did so, anyway.

Late Saturday afternoon of that week, she attended a wedding. Officer Joe Elrod was finally marrying his longtime girlfriend, Lindsey's hairdresser, Paula Campbell. Both Dan and Lindsey were invited, of course. She would have liked for them to have gone together—but that was expecting too much of Dan, she supposed. He hadn't even guaranteed that he would be home from his conference in time to attend. It depended, he said, on whether his flight into Little Rock was on time.

Resigned to going stag, she put on a colorful spring dress and a bright smile, and went to the wedding.

To her disappointment Dan didn't show for the ceremony. She sat with friends and made a pretense of being enthralled by the festivities. She was quite sure that no one watching her could tell that part of her simply wasn't there—the part she had given to Dan.

A reception at the Edstown country club followed the ceremony. Lindsey had been there only a few minutes when she was approached by Dan's sister, Tina.

"That brother of mine." Tina shook her head in disapproval. "Can you imagine him missing the wedding of one of his own officers? Honestly, I don't know what to do with that man."

"He said he would try to make it if he could. I suppose his flight was delayed."

Tina sighed. "Work always comes first with him."

"Now, you know that's not true. If you or Polly was in trouble, he would drop everything to be there for you."

"Oh, I know," Tina relented. "I'm just being a bossy older sister, I guess. I wish he had something besides work in his life." She suddenly brightened. "Maybe he's met someone in Dallas. Maybe that's what's keeping him there."

Lindsey felt her smile go stiff. It was all she could do to hold on to it.

Polly joined them then, all dimples and excitement. "Hi, Lindsey."

"Hi, Polly. How are you?"

"Fine, thank you. Wasn't that a beautiful wedding?"

"It was lovely." The reception was quite nice, as well. Very low-key and budget conscious, the emphasis was on friends and family gathered to share the newlyweds' joy. And judging from the beaming expressions on the faces of the bride and groom, it seemed there was quite a bit to celebrate.

"Oh, look. There's Uncle Dan."

Polly's cheery announcement made Lindsey's heart trip and then beat faster. It seemed like weeks, rather than days, since she'd last seen him. She turned eagerly, smiling when she saw him moving toward them. He looked so handsome in his dark suit.

He gave Lindsey a polite nod, then threw an arm around Polly's shoulders for an affectionate hug. "How's my favorite niece?"

She giggled. "You always say that. I'm your *only* niece."

"Mmm. But still my favorite." He turned then to his sister, dropping a light kiss on her cheek. "Hi, sis. You look very nice."

"Thank you." And then she was unable to resist adding reproachfully, "I missed seeing you at the wedding."

"My flight was delayed. I got here as soon as I could."

Lindsey was beginning to wonder if he'd completely forgotten her presence when he finally turned to her. "Hi, princess. How was the wedding?"

He spoke to her in the very same tone he'd used with Polly. As if, Lindsey thought, she was his second-favorite niece.

Even though she understood why he was being so circumspect, it still hurt a bit. "The wedding was very nice. How was your conference?"

"Not bad. Excuse me, I'd better go speak to the

bride and groom and offer my apologies for missing the ceremony.''

With that, he walked away. Without a backward glance.

''Well.'' Tina gazed after her brother with apparent bemusement. ''He's in an odd mood.''

''I didn't think so,'' Polly said, seeming surprised by the comment.

''I did. Did you notice, Lindsey?''

''Maybe he's just tired from his conference,'' Lindsey offered weakly.

''I suppose you're right. Oh, there's Donna—I've been wanting to talk to her about something. See you later, Lindsey.''

Polly dashed off, as well, joining a chattering group of teenagers in one corner of the ballroom. Lindsey was left alone.

She didn't stay that way long, of course. It was only moments later when a friend joined her, followed by a couple of others. But it still stung badly that Dan had practically brushed her off so easily, when she'd been so very pleased to see him.

He called her that night, a couple of hours after she arrived home from the reception. She had half expected him to drop by, but once again she was disappointed.

''Sorry we didn't get to talk more at the reception,'' he said.

She had to work a bit to keep the lingering hurt out of her voice. ''I was hoping we'd get to spend a little time together.''

''It was…awkward. With so many people there watching us and all.''

Lindsey didn't remember anyone actually watching them. She believed that more attention had actually been turned toward the bride and groom. She kept that opinion to herself, though, when she murmured, "I thought you might come by here tonight."

"I'm a little tired. And there might have been talk if my truck was seen in your driveway the very night I came home."

She was getting decidedly impatient with his paranoia about other people finding out about them. Would it really be so bad if they went public? Sure, there would be some talk at first, but then the novelty of the relationship would wear off. Attention would then turn to fresh, new gossip, and Lindsey and Dan could concentrate on themselves.

"So when will I see you?"

"I'll try to drop by tomorrow for a little while. Will you be home?"

"Yes," she said with a faint sigh. She would wait for him—just as she'd spent the past four days waiting for a phone call that had never come.

They wouldn't be able to go on this way much longer. At least, *she* wouldn't.

The one place Lindsey felt comfortable visiting Dan without arousing curiosity was in his office. She'd always spent considerable time there. Carrying her reporter's notebook, she charmed her way past Hazel on the following Wednesday afternoon with the excuse that she wanted to ask him about a home break-in that had happened the night before.

She did ask him about the break-in, of course, carefully recording his answers for a news article. She even argued with him a little when he wouldn't give her a list of the items stolen. He told her that was neither her business nor her readers'.

"What else is going on here?" she asked when they'd settled that touchy point.

He shrugged. "The usual. We're having some trouble with the McAllisters again. They got into another loud and violent altercation last night. I don't know why those two don't split up before one of them ends up killing the other. She's as bad as he is—they get to drinking and they turn mean."

"I suppose no one else would have either of them."

"You got that right."

She held her pencil poised above the pad. "Any other calls last night?"

"We're cooperating with the state police on a drug case that might have some connection here in town. There's nothing for you to print now, but I'll let you know if anything newsworthy goes down."

There'd been a time, she mused, when he wouldn't have given her even that much about an ongoing investigation. Maybe they *were* making some progress. "I hate to think about drug dealers coming into our little town."

His scowl was fierce. "They're going to have to get past me first."

Coming from someone else, the statement might have sounded like melodramatic bravado. But Dan had said the words simply and sincerely. He took his responsibilities very personally.

"That's all I've got for you today," he said, opening a folder on his desk. "Things have settled down a bit since Eddie's been locked up."

She closed her notebook. "Thanks for the update."

"What other big stories are you pursuing today?" he asked lightly, half his attention seeming to be on his paperwork.

She smiled. "Nothing earth shaking. They're opening the new wing of the hospital this afternoon. Six whole new rooms. I'll be there to hear Dr. Frank make a speech."

"I ran into Don Pettit this morning when I had breakfast at the Rainbow Café. Can't remember how it came up, but he mentioned you've changed your mind about putting your house on the market."

He'd spoken in an ultracasual tone, but Lindsey sensed that the comment wasn't quite as offhanded as he pretended. "I changed my mind because I've decided to stay in Edstown."

"It take it that means you've also changed your mind about pursuing a job in a bigger news venue? You talked about Dallas or Atlanta before."

Frowning, she studied his face, trying to read his unrevealing expression. "I know I talked about it, but that's all changed now."

"Maybe you should give it a little more thought before you make a final decision. How long are you going to be content writing articles about the usually mundane things that go on around here? You could be covering real news."

"Murders? Other serious crimes? Political scandals? Interviewing wheeler-dealers and tabloid celebrities, maybe? As interesting as that might be for a while, I'm quite content for now to write about small-town life.''

''You only moved back here a couple of years ago because your father needed you. I'd hate to think you were staying only because of a new sense of obligation.''

She didn't care for this conversation at all. ''I'm not *obligated* to stay here,'' she said firmly. ''I'm choosing to stay this time. There's a difference, you know.''

He didn't reply.

Turning the table on him, she said, ''You could be chief of police in a bigger market, you know. You'd have state-of-the-art police equipment, a highly trained force of officers, much more interesting crimes to investigate than a few home break-ins and domestic squabbles. Why are *you* staying?''

''That's different,'' he muttered.

''How?''

''I'm settled here. Have been for years. I'm sitting comfortably in a rut that I have no real desire to climb out of, even if I *was* confident that I could go anywhere I wanted. You're younger than I am, less rooted, more ambitious. I'd hate for you to have any regrets in years to come that you didn't go as far as you could have.''

She reminded herself that Dan had her welfare at heart. That his concern for her future and her happiness meant he really did care for her despite his awkwardness in expressing himself.

Which didn't mean that she liked having him sit there and all but urge her to move away.

She stood, deciding that this was the wrong time

and place to get into an in-depth discussion about their future. ''We can talk about this another time. We both have to get on with our work—mundane though it may be.''

''Look, Lindsey, I didn't mean to annoy you,'' he said, rising.

''I'm not annoyed,'' she lied. ''Just busy. See you later, okay?''

''Do that.''

She walked to the door and put her hand on the knob. ''And, Dan…?''

''Yeah?''

''Maybe you'd better decide if you really want me to stay,'' she said quietly.

She figured he knew as well as she did that they couldn't keep their relationship undefined and under wraps indefinitely.

Chapter Fourteen

It had been inevitable for the past twenty years that Dan would break Lindsey's heart. He'd come close to doing so numerous times. He had hurt her desperately when he'd married Melanie after giving Lindsey that memorable birthday kiss. But she'd allowed herself to get complacent this time. Maybe she just wanted so badly to believe things would work out that she wouldn't allow herself to consider any possibility.

She suspected her feelings for him were stronger than and deeper than his for her—but maybe she believed she had enough love and optimism for both of them.

It turned out she was wrong.

They lay in Dan's bed, wrapped snugly together, hearts still racing, and breathing still uneven from a particularly energetic bout of lovemaking. Dan should have been loose and relaxed—as Lindsey was—but she felt a certain tenseness in the muscles beneath her cheek.

She knew what his problem was. She'd shown up at his door this evening without an invitation, not really caring if any of the local gossips saw her there. Still stewing over their conversation in his office earlier that week, she'd decided it was time for one of them—and it looked as though it had to be her—to move their relationship forward.

Dan had looked worried about her arrival, but he hadn't turned her away, of course. The conversation she'd intended to initiate with him had been postponed when he kissed her. That kiss had led to another and then another—which had eventually led straight to his bedroom.

Now, she thought in exasperation, Dan was thinking about gossip again, wondering if anyone was speculating about why her car was parked in his driveway at this late hour, hoping no one would make anything of it. ''Chill out, will you? No one really cares about me being here.''

He chuckled, but it was a rather weak effort. ''You're underestimating the curiosity level of the average tattlemonger.''

''Everyone knows you and I are friends. There's nothing extraordinary about friends spending time together. For all anyone knows, we're in here eating popcorn and playing Scrabble.''

To her regret he slid out from under her and sat up, reaching for his clothes. ''Yeah, well, you'd still better head home soon. No one plays Scrabble and eats popcorn all night.''

She sighed as she began to dress. "Dan, don't you think it's about time for us to stop being so secretive? I mean, we've been together for several weeks now. Don't you think it's going to come out eventually?"

"I prefer not to have my private life discussed in the beauty parlor and the barber shop."

She raised herself to one elbow and propped her head on her hand. "I know you hate being gossiped about because of what happened with Melanie and all, but—"

She could almost feel an invisible wall go up between them. "Melanie is another subject I prefer not to discuss."

The flat rebuff stung. Surely she and Dan were going to have to talk about his ex-wife at some point. They couldn't spend the rest of their lives pretending the entire marriage had never happened. She needed to know how he felt about Melanie now. What she could do to help him get over the hurt and the betrayal. She desperately wanted to know how he felt about marrying again eventually—starting a family, maybe.

She'd spent a lot of time lately fantasizing about having a family with Dan.

"Couldn't we at least see a movie together or something?" she asked wistfully. "In a nice, friendly way, I mean. It's been weeks since I've been out."

There was a faint note of apology in his voice when he replied. "I suppose we could do that. We've certainly been to movies together before."

"Yes, we have."

"How about this Saturday night?"

"Saturday?" She winced, feeling rather foolish now. "I can't Saturday."

"Why not?"

"I have plans."

"Plans?" he repeated very casually. "What sort of plans?"

"It's a charity bowling tournament—raising money for juvenile arthritis research. I'm covering the event for the newspaper."

"You aren't bowling in the tournament?"

She laughed as she tugged her shirt over her head. "Heavens, no. I'm really a terrible bowler."

Fully dressed now, he stood half-turned away from her as he faced the mirror over his dresser and ran a hand through his hair. "Your private lessons didn't help?"

"Private—? Oh, you mean my date with Bo." Was he teasing or was that a hint of jealousy in his voice?

He nodded. "Is he going to be there Saturday night?"

"I don't know. I haven't talked to him lately." She slid her feet into her shoes, then reached up to smooth her own tousled hair.

Dan shoved his hands in his pockets and cleared his throat. "You know, there's no reason you shouldn't go out and have a good time occasionally. I certainly don't expect you to sit around at home waiting for a good time for us to be together."

She froze, one hand still in her hair. Very slowly she dropped her arm to her side. "Surely you aren't suggesting that I should go out with other men."

His face could have been carved from marble for

all the expression she could read there. ‘‘You just said yourself that you would like to get out more.’’

‘‘I meant with you.’’

He had to hear the emotions in her voice—the hurt, the disappointment. The disbelief. ‘‘Look, Lindsey—’’

Drawing herself up to her full five feet three inches, she crossed her arms over her chest and gazed unblinkingly at him. ‘‘You really wouldn’t mind if I go out again with Bo? Someone else, maybe?’’

‘‘I—’’

‘‘When were you planning to ask me out, Dan? On a real date, I mean. Or did you ever intend to appear in public with me?’’

‘‘Look, you know how I feel about my privacy.’’

‘‘Yes,’’ she whispered. ‘‘I know how you feel about that. What I don’t know is how you feel about me. About us.’’

He couldn’t seem to come up with an answer. He just stood there, looking at her with that inscrutable expression.

‘‘There has to be a reason you don’t want anyone to know about us,’’ she continued. ‘‘Is it because you don’t see a future for us? I’m just a secret affair for you until you get tired of me? Or maybe you’re already tired of me. Maybe that’s why you’ve been trying to convince me to date other men. Even to move away. Is that it, Dan?’’

‘‘You don’t understand. I’ve kept our affair a secret as much for your sake as for mine.’’

‘‘For *my* sake?’’ She might have laughed if she hadn’t been so upset.

‘‘Yes. You have a lot of friends in this town. People you admire and care about. I don't want it to be awkward for you here when—if this thing between us falls apart."

"*When* this thing falls apart. That's what you really mean, isn't it? You don't give us a chance, do you?"

"I'm just trying to be realistic. One of us has to be."

"And what does that mean?"

He was beginning to go on the defensive, which was obviously making him irritable. "We both know there's no guarantee that this will work out. With all the initial strikes against us, in addition to the usual pressures of a new relationship, it's quite likely that one or both of us will decide it would be better if we just go back to being friends."

She tightened her arms around herself. "I won't be the one to decide that."

Taking a step toward her, he spoke more gently. "You can't know that for certain. We're in new territory here. You could very well decide that reality isn't nearly as interesting or exciting as infatuation."

The word hit her with the force of a slap. "Infatuation?" she repeated carefully.

His expression turned wary again. "Maybe I phrased that badly. What I meant was—"

"I think I know exactly what you meant." Almost vibrating with temper, she glared at him, remembering the conversation with Riley that she now suspected Dan had overheard. "Are you under the impression that I still have a starry-eyed schoolgirl crush on you? You think I'm too dense or too naive to know the difference between love and infatuation?"

He seemed to pale a bit at her use of the *L* word—

which, of course, only made her angrier. ''I know I'm not an easy guy to be involved with,'' he offered. ''I work too much and I'm too settled in my rather dull routines, and I have a hard time showing my feelings. No one would blame you for getting bored with all that.''

She stamped her foot—then immediately regretted doing so because she didn't want him thinking of her as a temperamental kid. But he made her so furious. ''Damn it, I am *not* Melanie!'' she shouted. ''I hate her for what she put you through—but mostly I hate her because I'm the one having to deal with the aftermath. If you're afraid of getting involved again, afraid of being hurt again—say so! Don't you dare try to put it all off on me.''

''I'm just trying to be sensible,'' he muttered without quite meeting her eyes.

She had never been so hurt or so angry in her entire adult life. ''You never intended to tell anyone about us, did you? You let me chase you—let me make a fool out of myself over you—and then you decided to humor me until I...what? Outgrew the crush I had on you? Got bored and moved on in search of bigger, better adventures? After all, an immature, empty-headed little princess like me couldn't possibly know what she really wants, right? It was up to you, the responsible, mature, *sensible* one to make sure neither of us would be embarrassed when I realized my terrible mistake.''

His narrowed brown eyes snapped with barely suppressed emotion. ''You aren't being fair.''

''Well, excuse me if I'm not in the mood to protect your tender feelings!'' Pausing in the doorway, she turned to fire one parting shot. ''Congratulations, Dan. You've finally accomplished something I've been trying to do for the past twenty years. Thanks to you, I can finally, wholeheartedly say that I'm completely over you.''

It seemed like a pretty good exit line. She decided she'd better make her escape before she ruined it by bursting into tears.

She would have the rest of her life to cry over him.

Dan had always found peace fishing. The lapping of the water against the sides of the boat. The call of birds overhead. The soft wind against his face. The quiet—no phones, computers, fax machines. He wore a pager on his belt, but that would go off only in an emergency.

He should have been completely relaxed. Content. But, as his companion on this particular outing observed, he was neither.

''Want to talk about it?'' Cameron asked casually, keeping his eyes focused on his fishing line.

Wearing a battered fishing cap Dan had once given him, Cameron had shown up at Dan's door on this Sunday afternoon and all but kidnapped him. Dan had been increasingly antisocial during the past couple of weeks, spending less time at his office and more time at home alone, which had probably caused some talk around town. He hadn't seen Lindsey since she'd walked out on him just over two weeks ago—didn't even know where she was, for certain. She'd left town with no more than a message for him that he wasn't to worry about her. That she would be just fine.

He wasn't so sure the same could be said about him.

He had initially resisted Cameron's fishing invitation, thinking he'd rather spend the time holed up by himself, but Cameron had been insistent. Dan had ended up in this boat almost before he knew it, not quite certain how his friend had accomplished the feat.

"Talk about what?" he asked, his tone as offhanded as Cameron's.

"Whatever's been eating you the past couple of weeks. I gotta tell you, man, your hang-dog expression is breaking my heart."

Though Cameron had spoken teasingly, Dan sensed that he was somewhat serious. He sighed. "Hell, Cam, I wouldn't know how to begin," he muttered.

"Let me get you started. You and Lindsey had a major falling out, right?"

Wincing at the sound of her name, Dan nodded grimly. "We had a pretty serious quarrel. Did she tell you about it?"

And if she had, just how much had she told him?

"No," Cameron replied. "She didn't tell me anything specifically. She just asked for some time off and said she had some things to work out. She looked so miserable that I couldn't help worrying about her. Marjorie asked me later if Lindsey had mentioned you when she asked for the leave of absence. That got me thinking—Marjorie's pretty perceptive, you know."

"Yes, I'm well aware of that." Actually, the last time he'd seen her he'd had the feeling that Marjorie could read him all too well.

Cameron worked his bait a bit, then let it settle

again. ‘‘You and I haven’t talked much about my life before I moved here, have we?’’

‘‘Not a lot.’’ Dan knew that Cameron had suffered an unhappy childhood—his parents had been wealthy but abusive. He’d worked as a reporter in Dallas for several years, ending up in Edstown when his pursuit of a juicy political exposé had made him enemies who’d beaten him and left him for dead on a little-traveled rural road. Serena had found him there, battered, broken and suffering a head injury that had robbed him of his memory for a time. Cameron had fallen in love with Serena, married her and left his former life behind so completely that he hardly ever mentioned it, maintaining only a few ties with close friends in Texas, who sometimes visited him here, since he rarely went back. ‘‘You still haven’t recovered all your memories, have you?’’

‘‘I’ll probably never get some of them back,’’ Cameron confirmed. ‘‘There are pretty big gaps in my past—most of which I would probably just as soon leave alone. There are a few memories that have returned to haunt me, though. Mistakes I made that I wish I could forget again.’’

Dan wondered where this was leading. ‘‘Er…I’m sure everyone has things in their past they’d rather not think about. I certainly have.’’ His ill-advised marriage, for one.

‘‘One of the worst mistakes I ever made involved a longtime friend. Her name was Amber. We went to high school together and remained in the same circle of friends for years afterward. Our gang used to get together at least once a week to visit and play games, watch movies and just hang out. You've met some of them when they've visited me here.''

''Yeah. They all seem nice. I don't remember meeting Amber, though.''

''No, you never met her. Her last name was Wallace. Sound familiar?''

Dan frowned. Wallace was the surname Cameron had selected apparently at random when he couldn't remember his own name. A Freudian coincidence, perhaps?

''Amber and I made the huge mistake of trying to turn our friendship into something more,'' Cameron continued. ''She sort of initiated it, but I didn't resist too much. She was pretty and amusing, and we obviously had a great deal in common. But that was all there was between us, I'm afraid. And it wasn't enough.''

Grimacing, Dan suddenly realized exactly where this was headed. ''Uh, Cam…''

''Needless to say, it was a disaster. I hurt her very badly, and I've never forgiven myself completely for doing so.''

Dan squirmed on the boat seat. ''I'm sure you didn't intentionally hurt her,'' he muttered, remembering the shattered look in Lindsey's eyes when she walked away from him.

''No. But that wasn't an excuse. I knew better all along than to get involved with her and to let her start making plans for us.''

Dan nodded glumly. ''Mistaking friendship for love usually does lead to heartache.''

''Especially when only one of the two is in love,''

Cameron agreed. ''And the other is operating under a delusion.''

''Whatever happened to Amber? Do you know?''

''Yeah. She moved out West, met someone else and got married. I've heard she's happy. She deserves to be.''

Dan swallowed hard. Would he be as happy for Lindsey if she announced plans to marry someone else? He hoped he would—but he doubted it. ''Is there a point to this story?'' he asked, to get that disturbing image out of his mind.

''Sorry if I'm stepping over the line here, but I thought you could use someone to talk to. I know it helped me to talk to my friend Shane after Amber and I broke up.''

''I appreciate it, but—''

''You and Lindsey did get involved, didn't you?''

Dan heaved a heavy sigh. ''Yeah.''

''I thought so. Now you're hating yourself for hurting her.''

Maybe Cameron really did understand. ''Yeah. That pretty well sums it up.''

''Believe me, I know how you feel. You probably feel the same way I did about Amber. I was very fond of her—but I just couldn't love her the way she wanted me to.''

Dan frowned. ''Well, no, that's not—''

''She was crazy about me—or at least, she thought she was. She started hinting about marriage and babies and growing old together—and I broke into a cold sweat. I guess you know that feeling.''

Actually, the thought of marrying Lindsey and having babies with her didn't scare Dan at all. It was the possibility that she would change her mind just as he allowed himself to start believing in that future that terrified him.

Funny. He and Melanie had never talked about the future. Other than one significant episode, they'd never seriously discussed having a family. Maybe they'd both known subconsciously from the beginning that theirs was not a till-death-do-us-part commitment.

"I imagine Lindsey will get over you—eventually," Cameron continued. "She'll realize someday that it wasn't her fault that you didn't love her. She's just not your type, that's all. The same way Amber wasn't my type."

"Cam, you've got it backward."

Cameron raised an eyebrow. "Surely you don't expect me to believe Lindsey's the one who changed her mind and dumped you."

"Well, no." *At least, not yet,* he added mentally.

"I didn't think so. Lindsey's not the love-'em-and-leave-'em type. She's too centered and levelheaded—something I noticed almost as soon as I met her. Because she's so petite and cute and ebullient, there's a tendency to underestimate her. But she's a woman who knows what she wants and doesn't change her mind on a whim."

"She's still young."

"Twenty-six? Hardly a child."

Absorbed in his thoughts, Dan missed a strike. The fish weren't biting worth a damn, and he'd missed the first bite he'd gotten.

"Don't torment yourself, Dan," Cameron advised kindly. "As you said, she's still young. She'll get over you eventually. Just as Amber got on with her life without me—though Amber probably doesn't take things as hard as Lindsey does. Amber's a little more flighty. She tends to romanticize everything—including me. She tried to believe I was someone I wasn't. You can't say the same about Lindsey. Not the way you two fuss and scrap over your jobs. She definitely knows your flaws, but she must have decided they didn't overshadow your strengths.''

Okay, Dan knew Lindsey was all too familiar with his flaws. She'd called him a stubborn, pigheaded, uncooperative, dictatorial workaholic so many times he could clearly hear her voice saying those words in his head right then.

She didn't romanticize him. But she'd decided she wanted him, anyway. And he'd driven her away.

Cameron reeled in his lure and cast toward a more promising-looking spot. ''I was incredibly fortunate to find Serena after that fiasco with Amber. I really didn't think I'd ever find anyone I could love like that. Amber was a fine woman, but she wasn't the right one for me. I'm sure you feel pretty much the same way about Lindsey. You see? I know exactly how you feel. I hope that helps you.''

''Cam?''

''Yeah?''

''Shut up.''

''Too much?''

''Yeah.''

Cameron jerked his hand back to set the hook when a fish finally took his bait. ''I never was much of a confidant. But I'm a hell of a fisherman,'' he said as he reeled in a nice-size crappie.

"Actually, I think you're underestimating one of your talents and overestimating another," Dan drawled. "But you've given me a lot to think about."

Cameron grinned. "That's going to be tough—as underequipped as you are for heavy thinking."

Before Dan could come up with a suitably sarcastic reply, a fish hit his own lure. Relieved to have an excuse to change the subject, he concentrated on landing the small bass. He knew he would spend plenty of time later mulling over the things Cameron had said.

Lindsey had always loved watching spring come to the Ozarks. The rolling hills on the horizon looked as though they'd been painted in soft-green watercolors. Pink-and-white dogwoods dotted the landscape, while fluffy white clouds floated lazily across a vivid-blue sky. Glittering lake water lapped against the rocky shore where she stood, stirred by a floral-scented breeze that kissed her cheek and toyed with her hair.

She was staying in a fishing cabin nestled on the edge of a picturesque mountain lake. The cabin belonged to Riley's uncle Bud, and it had been Riley who had offered it to Lindsey for a few weeks. Bud had insisted he wouldn't be visiting his own place anytime soon. He and Riley had both urged Lindsey to take a vacation, speculating aloud that overwork and exhaustion were the cause of her recent depression.

Without correcting them, she'd gratefully accepted the offer.

If she had any artistic talent, she would try to capture this scene on canvas. As it was, she had to commit it to memory instead. In the future, when she desperately needed solace, she would think about this place, this time, and hope it would bring her peace.

She huddled more snugly into her lightweight denim jacket, her hands buried in the lined pockets. It wasn't a particularly cool breeze that blew against her, but it made her shiver, anyway. She'd had trouble feeling warm enough lately. Actually, she'd been cold ever since Dan had accused her of being foolishly infatuated with him. Those staggeringly insensitive words had left a heart-deep chill she wasn't sure would ever go away completely.

How could he know her so well and yet remain so completely clueless?

The words she'd thrown at him as she'd left his bedroom echoed in her mind, almost drowning out the sounds of water and birds and rustling new leaves. *Congratulations, Dan. You've finally accomplished something I've been trying to do for the past twenty years. Thanks to you, I can finally, wholeheartedly say that I'm completely over you.*

What a lie that had been. Pure bravado. She would never be completely over him. But she would survive. She'd put her house on the market, get a job in some big, anonymous city and make a new life for herself, just as she had planned to do before she'd made the stupid mistake of letting herself believe Dan was starting to feel about her the way she'd felt about him for so long.

If there was one thing she had learned during the past few years, it was that she was fully capable of taking care of herself. She didn't need a man in her life—especially one so thickheaded that he couldn't tell the difference between an infatuated schoolgirl and a woman who loved him.

On that resolute note she turned to go back to the cabin—only to find herself standing face-to-face with that same obstinate male.

Chapter Fifteen

Silhouetted against the spring pastels of the woods behind him, Dan looked dark and almost forbidding as he stood there on the rocky path glowering at her. He didn't look particularly happy to see her. She wondered why he'd even gone to the trouble of finding her. "What are you doing here?"

He probably hadn't expected her to throw herself into his arms, but he seemed a bit taken aback by the gruffness of her greeting. Maybe he'd expected her to show a bit more surprise at his sudden appearance. While she hadn't been expecting him, she wasn't overly startled by his arrival. If nothing else, he would feel obligated to check up on her—his big-brother act that annoyed her so greatly.

"I had a hell of a time finding you," he growled without answering her question. "You could have told someone where you were going."

"Riley knew," she said with a shrug.

"Riley wasn't talking. He said you deserved your privacy. What if your brother had wanted to reach you?"

"I have my laptop with me. I check my e-mail occasionally. B.J. knows he can reach me that way. So, how did you find me?"

"Marjorie took pity on me and got the information from Riley. He couldn't turn her down, of course."

"Few people can." She shoved her hands more deeply into her pockets and met his gaze without blinking. "You still haven't told me why you're here."

He glanced over his shoulder, toward the modest little cabin that was just visible through the trees. "Why don't we go inside where we can have some coffee or something and talk?"

The cabin was very small. Cozy. The lights dim and intimate. "I'd rather stay out here."

"You look cold."

"It isn't any warmer inside. What do you want to say?"

He studied her expression for several moments before speaking. "You aren't being very encouraging."

"You expected me to blush and giggle like the silly schoolgirl you think I am?"

For a moment she thought he was going to accuse her of being unfair again. Maybe she was—but she felt she deserved a few shots in return for the terrible unjustness of his doubts about her.

Instead he drew a deep breath and stepped past her, stopping at the water's edge. Gazing at the mountains in the distance, he spoke without looking around at her. ''You're still pretty mad at me, huh?''

It was such a typically dense, utterly male thing to say that all she could do was stare at his back in wholly feminine exasperation. ''Yeah,'' she said finally. ''I'm still mad.''

''I hurt your feelings.''

A fist-size rock lay right beside the toe of her sneaker. She considered picking it up and throwing it at him—just for the satisfaction of it. But since she wasn't really a violent person, she contented herself with saying simply, ''You broke my heart.''

''I wasn't trying to break your heart. I was trying to keep mine from being broken.''

''Oh, please,'' she muttered, stiffening. Was he going to try to convince her now that he'd really cared? After the things he'd said to her that night?

''Lindsey—''

She shook her head forcefully. ''Do we have to go through this again? Didn't we say everything there was to say when I left your house?''

''No. There were a few things that didn't get said.''

''You wanted to tell me then that you were trying to keep your heart from being broken again?''

''I didn't say again. Melanie bruised my ego. Humiliated me. Infuriated me. But she didn't break my heart—it was never hers to break.''

He had refused to talk about his ex-wife before. Why was he suddenly willing to do so now? Just what was he trying to tell her? How much was he willing to share, now that he'd brought the subject up? ''If you weren't in love with her, then why did you marry her?''

"Because she told me she was pregnant."

Stunned, Lindsey reached up slowly to brush her breeze-tossed hair out of her eyes. "I never knew that."

He shrugged. "She told me the night of your birthday party. On our way back to her place, actually. She convinced me to elope with her, and I stupidly agreed it was the right thing to do. A couple of weeks later I realized we'd made a mistake. Several of them, actually."

"She wasn't pregnant."

"No."

"But she told you she was—the night of my party?" She remembered how angry Melanie had been that Dan had danced with Lindsey, that he'd given her that birthday kiss afterward. Surely Melanie hadn't decided then to...

"Yeah. That night." Dan turned a stone over with the toe of his boot. "I tried to make it work. But maybe I didn't try hard enough. Maybe if I'd worked as hard at my marriage as I did at my career, Melanie wouldn't have been so bored and dissatisfied that she turned to having affairs and pilfering cash to keep her entertained."

"That wasn't your fault. Melanie had a reckless streak. B.J. always said so."

"Maybe that's what drew me to her initially. The old opposites-attract principle. But I don't think I would have let that attraction lead to marriage if it hadn't been for...well—"

"If she hadn't told you she was pregnant."

He nodded, still without looking around.

"Were you very disappointed?" she asked quietly. "About the pregnancy, I mean."

"No. To be honest, I was relieved. I told myself I just wasn't ready for fatherhood. Truth was, I wasn't eager to have a child with Melanie. I never was."

Lindsey drew a deep breath. "I'm sorry things went so badly between you and Melanie. But I still don't appreciate you comparing me to her. I had no intention of trapping you into marriage. And I would never have betrayed you the way she did."

"I've never compared you to Melanie. I just didn't want to get involved in another relationship for the wrong reasons."

It hurt to hear him say that. To hide her emotions, she walked to the water's edge and idly picked up a small, flat stone. "Because you think I'm merely infatuated with you?"

"It seemed like a distinct possibility to me. And I wasn't the only one who worried about that," he added a bit defensively.

She let the stone go, watching it skip four or five times across the surface of the water before it finally sank. "You could have discussed your concerns with me. Or you could have trusted me to know my own mind."

"There was just too much at stake this time."

"Because I'm B.J.'s sister. Too many connections. And you were probably feeling protective toward me. Afraid I would be hurt."

"All of that is true," he conceded. "But mostly I was afraid the infatuation would wear off. That *I* would be hurt. Because I never mistook my own feelings for infatuation."

Her fingers closed tightly around another small stone. ‘‘What did you feel for me?’’

‘‘The same thing I feel now. I love you.’’

The stone fell from her suddenly limp hand, landing with a soft plop in the water at her toes. ‘‘Like a little sister?’’

‘‘I haven’t thought of you as a little sister since the first time I kissed you. Probably for some time before that. I just wouldn’t admit it—not even to myself.’’

She blinked rapidly in a futile attempt to hold back a wave of tears. ‘‘Then you love me?’’

Though she wasn’t looking at him, she heard him swallow before answering, ‘‘Yes.’’

She turned then, finding him watching her with an anxious expression that twisted her heart. ‘‘How can you love me when you don’t trust me?’’

‘‘I would trust you with my life,’’ he answered firmly. ‘‘But I was afraid to trust you with my heart. It took me a while to get past that cowardice. But I’ve done a lot of thinking, and I know what I want now. More than anything I’ve ever wanted.’’

‘‘You aren’t afraid now?’’

‘‘Maybe a little,’’ he admitted. ‘‘But I’m willing to take the risk—if you still are.’’

‘‘What…?’’ she had to stop to clear her throat. ‘‘What made you change your mind?’’

‘‘I missed you too much to risk losing you forever,’’ he answered simply. ‘‘I haven’t been able to sleep since you’ve been gone. I couldn’t eat. Damn it, I couldn’t even work.’’

That made her eyebrows rise. ‘‘That’s a shock.’’

‘‘It was to my staff, too,’’ he admitted with just the faintest touch of wry humor. His half smile faded almost as soon as it appeared. ''When you left me, you told me you were over me. I can't blame you for being mad at me. I was a dumb jerk, and I hurt you badly by treating you so insensitively. All I'm asking is a chance to win you back. I'd like to take you out on dates. In public. I want to court you the way I should have from the beginning. Will you give me that chance, Lindsey?''

Her breath caught in her throat, temporarily preventing her from answering.

He took a step toward her. ''I'm prepared to beg, if necessary.''

That loosened her voice. ''No, *please* don't do that. I'm trying very hard not to cry.''

He frowned. ''Is that good or bad?''

She swiped at her eyes with the back of her hand. ''I hate to cry. It makes my face all red and splotchy.''

''You'd still be beautiful to me,'' he assured her.

A watery giggle escaped her. ''Okay, don't overdo the courtship stuff. All I wanted from you was your trust, not a bunch of flowery compliments.''

''I meant it, you know.''

The smile that accompanied his words was so sweet that her eyes filled again. ''Stop that. Right now,'' she ordered a bit desperately.

For the first time since she'd turned to find him standing behind her, he reached out to touch her. He wiped a tear from her cheek with the tips of his fingers. ''You still haven't given me an answer. Is it too late?''

''I've been in love with you for most of my life,''

she whispered, gazing up at him. ''It would've taken me a lot more than a few weeks to get over you.''

He cupped her face between his hands—and once again she felt this very strong man tremble. His lips brushed hers lightly, gently. Almost reverently.

But that wasn't what she wanted from him. She wrapped her arms around his neck and tugged him down to her, rising on tiptoes to crush her mouth against his.

He responded with a fervor that he must have been barely holding in check until then. He pulled her so high into his arms that her toes dangled above the ground. His tongue slipped between her lips, and she eagerly welcomed him back.

She'd known she missed him, but only now did she realize exactly how empty she had been. It was as if she'd been in stasis—and was only now coming back to life. She could almost feel the warmth spreading through her body again, tingling in her fingers and toes, pooling deep inside her.

It felt so good to be fully alive again.

''Can we go inside now?'' he murmured against her lips. ''I really am too old to make love on a beach. At least without an air mattress.''

She giggled into his mouth. ''Would you stop with the old-guy routine? You aren't even forty yet.''

''Okay, I'm a mere kid. But I still don't want these rocks cutting into my bare—''

She covered his mouth with hers again. When she finally released him, they were already moving toward the cabin.

* * *

Dan was true to his word when they returned to Edstown. He courted her. Publicly.

He called. He sent flowers. He brought candy. He took her out to eat. To the movies. To official functions. He did everything but hire an airplane to write across the sky that he was dating her. He rarely spent an entire night with her—that, he said, would have caused too much negative talk about her—but he no longer tried to keep it a secret that there was more between them than friendship these days.

After the initial buzz of interest, their friends and neighbors had accepted the relationship quite well. They weren't quite as surprised as Lindsey might have expected. Apparently, she hadn't been as discreet about her feelings for Dan as she'd thought, during the past couple of years.

There were some who expressed mild amazement that Dan was being quite so attentive to her. He'd always been so careful to keep his personal life private. Even during his marriage to Melanie, he'd spent more time on the job than at home. That was changing now. He was even starting to take off weekends, though his pager and radio were never far from his hand, of course.

Lindsey should have been deliriously happy. She couldn't quite understand why she wasn't.

"Everything's going okay with you and Dan?" her brother asked during a telephone call early in May.

"Oh, sure. Things are great," Lindsey assured him heartily. B.J. was one of those who had expressed no surprise about Lindsey's feelings for Dan, but found it a little harder to believe that Dan was equally committed. It wasn't that people who knew him thought of Dan as cold or hardhearted. He was just known for being very reserved. Extremely reticent about expressing his feelings. And, of course, a hard-line law enforcer with a deep-seated wariness of the media.

Lindsey couldn't blame anyone for expecting a few conflicts to crop up between her and Dan. She told herself it was ridiculous that it bothered her that no such problems *had* occurred.

"This really is great, you know," B.J. said. "I know you've had a thing for Dan for a long time, and I'm glad he's finally realized you belong together. I spoke to him yesterday, and he seems very committed to this relationship."

Almost relentlessly committed, Lindsey was tempted to add. Dan seemed to be working harder at this relationship than he had at anything in a long time. If this was meant to be, should it really be so hard for him?

She didn't share her concerns with her brother, but chatted amicably for another few minutes about other subjects before they disconnected. B.J. promised to get home as soon as he could for a visit. Lindsey warmly urged him to do so. As she hung up the phone, she told herself she was being uncharacteristically apprehensive and pessimistic to wonder if she and Dan would still be together when B.J. arrived.

She was kept late at the newspaper office the next day, arriving home at almost six-thirty. Dan was already there. He even had dinner started. He greeted her with a smile and a kiss. She couldn't help noticing that he looked tired, even though he'd put in a shorter day at the office than usual. "Hi. Running late today, I see," he said.

''Mmm. Early day for you?''

''No, I left at the usual time. Just after five.''

Lindsey shook her head. ''Since when is eight to five a 'usual' day for you?''

''Since I decided to set different priorities in my life,'' he replied, popping a slice of carrot into her mouth.

She crunched and swallowed, then said, ''You know, I really don't mind if you work late sometimes. I tend to have long hours, myself, as I'm sure you've noticed. I certainly don't want to interfere with your job.''

He shrugged and turned back to the stove. ''I'm handling it.''

''*When* are you handling it?'' she insisted. ''You're spending so much time with me you must have cut your work hours by at least a third. I'm not complaining about the amount of time we're together, of course, but I don't want your duties to suffer.''

''I said I'm handling it,'' he said, and it was as close to snapping as he'd come since that day at the fishing cabin. He drew a deep breath and sent her another smile. ''Sorry. I didn't mean that to come out so abruptly.''

That was another problem she was having with him, she mused. He was just too darned polite lately. She felt almost as if she needed to apologize in return, for some reason.

''I'm going to go wash up,'' she said, turning toward the doorway. ''I'll be back in a minute to help you finish dinner.''

''I've got it under control if you'd like to rest awhile. I'll call you when it's ready.''

She gave him a smile that felt a bit too toothy and left the room before she could say anything imprudent.

What was the matter with her, anyway? Splashing cold water on her face in the bathroom, she wondered if she was losing her mind. For at least half her life, she'd fantasized about being with Dan. Now that she was, she kept feeling that something was wrong.

She couldn't quite put her finger on the problem. He was being the perfect lover. Attentive, polite, thoughtful.

Maybe that was what was wrong, she thought with a frown. The Dan she'd always loved wasn't known for being any of those things. This one sort of unnerved her.

Over dinner she tried again to get him to talk about work. She even asked him a few pointed questions about an on-going investigation. The old Dan would have flatly informed her that the answers were none of her business. Instead he gave her the information and then asked her politely not to print it without an official release.

She sighed and finished her dinner, telling herself that only a crazy woman would be upset because the man she loved was being so nice to her.

Dan must have fallen asleep at his desk. It seemed that one minute he'd been peering blearily at a computer printout and the next minute someone was shaking his shoulder, bringing him out of a very bizarre dream. Something about being buried under piles of paperwork, he thought.

Rubbing his eyes, he looked up expecting to see

his secretary frowning over him. He was startled to find Lindsey glowering at him instead. "What are you doing here?" he asked blankly. "It's only..."

He glanced at his watch, trying to focus on the dial.

"Five o'clock in the morning," she supplied for him in a voice cold enough to freeze coffee. "And the reason I'm here is to tell you that you're a jerk. A stupid, stubborn, chauvinistic, macho jerk."

"I'm not chauvinistic." He eyed the familiar flush of temper on her face, wondering what he'd done to set her off this time. He'd been so very careful lately. He hadn't argued with her, hadn't neglected her. He'd given her compliments, flowers, gifts. What had he done wrong? "How did you know I was here, anyway?"

Her arms were locked tightly across her chest, her green eyes sparking with anger. "I've recently discovered that you've been working in the middle of the nights and coming in early in the mornings to catch up on all the work you've been neglecting so you could indulge me."

"Who told you that?" He was really going to have to talk to Hazel about discussing his business outside the office, he decided.

"That's none of your concern. It doesn't matter, anyway. Beginning right now, you're free to go back to your former schedule. You can work all you like, and when you aren't working you'll have a little extra time to rest since you won't have to worry about entertaining me."

"I'm not sure what you're trying to say," he muttered, pushing a hand through his hair and rising slowly to his feet.

She took a step backward. ''I think I'm making myself quite clear,'' she snapped. ''It's over, Dan. You and I are finished. I'm breaking up with you.''

With that lofty pronouncement, she spun on one heel and stamped toward the door.

Dan caught her just as her hand touched the doorknob. Pulling her away, he locked the door and stood in front of it, blocking her exit with his body. ''What the hell are you talking about?''

''I'm talking about this condescending and incredibly insulting game you've been playing with me!''

He winced. For such a small woman, she could certainly make a lot of noise when she gave it an effort. ''Damn it, Lindsey, I haven't been playing any games with you. You know me better than that.''

She made a sound that came perilously close to an indelicate snort. ''I used to know you. I don't anymore. And apparently you don't know me at *all.*''

Deep inside him, panic began to stir. As many times as he'd seen Lindsey in a temper—and that was more times than he could begin to count—he'd never seen her eyes look so hard. ''You're mad because I've been spending so much time at the office after I leave you?'' he asked tentatively. ''Do you want us to spend more nights together?''

He got a clue that it had been the wrong thing to ask when she gave a low, almost feral growl and reached out to tug at his arm. ''Move out of my way,'' she ordered. ''Let me out of here.''

Pressing his back against the door, he shook his head. ''I'm not letting you walk out like this. Not until I understand exactly what I've done wrong.

Damn it, I've done everything I can to make you happy. Tell me what else you want me to do.''

Giving up on the physical impossibility of moving him, she settled for making a fist and punching his shoulder. ''I don't *need* you to make me happy. I'm perfectly capable of doing that for myself. I have a great job, a nice home, a lot of friends. I wanted you to be my partner in life, not my caretaker. But you couldn't give me enough credit for that.''

Her eyes glittered with tears now, and he sensed she was making a massive effort to hold them back. Feeling like the jerk she'd called him, he offered lamely, ''I'm sorry. I thought—''

''I know what you thought,'' she cut in after drawing a deep breath to steady herself. ''You thought I was like Melanie. Needy and selfish and clingy and jealous...''

''No!''

''Yes,'' she insisted. ''You were afraid you'd ruin another relationship by being yourself, so you changed. But I never asked you to change. I never wanted you to. I tried to change myself for you at one time, and I realized then it would never work. I needed you to want me just the way I am. And that's all I ever wanted of you.''

Her use of the past tense was ripping his heart out. There had to be a way to fix this, he assured himself somewhat desperately. He couldn't bear it if it ended like this.

''You won't even fight with me anymore,'' she added a bit plaintively.

Releasing the tight rein he'd been keeping on his emotions, he caught her forearms in his hands and jerked her toward him, bending so that his face was very close to hers. ''You want a fight? Then try again to leave this office. I love you, Lindsey Gray, and I'm not going to let you walk away from me after all you've put me through to get to this point.''

''All I've put *you* through? I—''

''Be quiet.''

She blinked at the sharpness of his voice—a tone she hadn't heard since they'd become lovers.

''I do not—I repeat, *I do not*—think you are anything like Melanie. Maybe I've gone a little overboard trying to make this relationship work, but that's only because you mean more to me than anyone or anything in my entire life—and that includes my job. I wanted everything to be perfect between us—but maybe I was trying to make it a little too perfect. You said you've never wanted me to change, and I understand that, because I wouldn't change one thing about you. Not your temper or your stubbornness, or your impulsiveness or your occasional unreasonableness.''

Ignoring her affronted gasp, he reiterated, ''I wouldn't change a thing. *I love you.*''

''I love you, too,'' she whispered. ''Just the way you are—the way you've always been. I've always loved you.''

''I think the problem is that we've been trying to divide ourselves between too many places. If we lived in the same place, slept in the same bed every night, then we wouldn't feel the need to try to cram so much into the hours we spend together.''

''You want us to live together?''

"I want us to get married," he answered firmly. "I've just been waiting for the right time to ask you."

She gave him a suspicious look that might have been amusing under different circumstances. "If I say yes, will you stop acting so weird? Will you treat me like an equal again, and not like a fragile, overly sensitive child?"

"I'll treat you like my wife," he answered simply, feeling his lungs beginning to work correctly again. "My partner."

For the first time since she'd awakened him, she smiled. "I like the sound of that."

"Wait a minute," he said when she would have moved closer to him. "You've got to make a promise, yourself."

"To love, honor and cherish until death do us part?"

"Well, yes—but also to let me know when I'm acting 'weird.' If you'd just said something days ago, we could have avoided several days of misunderstanding."

She frowned thoughtfully. "You're right," she said, as if the notion had never occurred to her. "I guess I was acting weird, too. I didn't want to risk messing everything up, either."

"You see?" Satisfied, he tugged her into his arms. "Let's get weird together," he suggested, then smothered her giggle with his mouth.

It probably wasn't the most romantic proposal in history, he thought, as Lindsey wrapped herself around him and returned the embrace with the passion he loved about her. She didn't want flowery phrases and romantic gestures from him. She just wanted *him,* exactly the way he was.

That was the easiest gift of all to offer her.

* * * * *

Look out for the last instalment of
HOT OFF THE PRESS *with*
Dateline Matrimony.

On sale September 2002.